THE GOOD WOMAN'S HIRED HAND

A 20TH CENTURY WESTERN ROMANCE

Paul Gaines
Marjorie Anderson

PAUL GAINES AND MARJORIE ANDERSON

outskirtspress
DENVER, COLORADO

This is a work of fiction. The events and characters described herein are imaginary and are not intended to refer to specific places or living persons. The opinions expressed in this manuscript are solely the opinions of the author and do not represent the opinions or thoughts of the publisher. The author has represented and warranted full ownership and/or legal right to publish all the materials in this book.

The German Woman's Hired Hand
A 20th Century Western Romance
All Rights Reserved.
Copyright © 2014 Paul Gaines and Marjorie Anderson
v3.0

Cover Photo © 2014 thinkstockphotos.com. All rights reserved - used with permission.

This book may not be reproduced, transmitted, or stored in whole or in part by any means, including graphic, electronic, or mechanical without the express written consent of the publisher except in the case of brief quotations embodied in critical articles and reviews.

Outskirts Press, Inc.
http://www.outskirtspress.com

ISBN: 978-1-4787-4091-9

Outskirts Press and the "OP" logo are trademarks belonging to Outskirts Press, Inc.

PRINTED IN THE UNITED STATES OF AMERICA

Dedication

Paul Gaines and Marjorie Anderson dedicate this collaboration of their efforts to Paul's wife, Nancy (Stogner) Gaines, without whose counsel, suggestions, extensive typing of Paul's yellow pad longhand and countless hours of proofing, "The German Woman's Hired Hand" would never have seen print. In her honor, the character of Rev. Eli Steigner bears her maiden name in its authentic German spelling.

Prologue

It was the spring of 1942. Seventeen year-old Jacob Martin Sorrells was riding out the front gate of the Baptist Boys Ranch in Century, Wyoming. He had just graduated from the local high school, one of the few residents of the institution to do so. Jacob "Jake" Sorrells was on his way to enlist in the Army Air Corp. Driving the ancient truck as it rattled its way to town was Lester "Buck" Thomas, the ranch foreman and one of the few people young Sorrells considered a friend. In one way or the other Jake Sorrells had performed almost every job at the ranch under Buck's supervision.

His relationship with Thomas had gone back to when Jake was nine years old and had been assigned to help clean out stalls in the milking barn. At the time Jake Sorrells had been at the Ranch three years. Buck Thomas had found the boy quiet, quick to learn and mentally tough. Always willing to take on any task and see it through. More than once Jake and Buck had weathered the Wyoming winters moving or feeding the ranch's cattle and its few horses. Jake Sorrells, Buck often said, seemed more at ease around animals than he did with people.

In high school he was, for the most part, a good student, again quick to learn, and in athletics where he excelled, he had been "coachable." He had not been the tallest or the fastest but he made up for any physical shortcomings with a fierce determination to push himself to the limit of his ability. In the process he had lettered at every sport the school offered and most of the time proved to be the best athlete. Buck had attended almost every one of his games, in some ways making up for the fact that, unlike all the other boys, there was never a father figure for Jake. He didn't require one.

"The kid is a survivor," was how Buck described his young ward. It was fitting that Buck go with Jake to the draft board and to sign the necessary papers for his enlistment. It was seven months after Pearl Harbor and soon Jake Sorrells would be in basic training, where again he would excel. Other young men would hate the army, hate the regiment and the physical stress of basic training. Jake Sorrells loved it. The army, he thought, was not too different from anything else in his life. The army fed him, clothed him and gave him a place to sleep. What else could anyone ask for? He had really never owned anything and didn't want to. A few months later he was on a troop ship headed for England and even more training.

Chapter One
Jake for Hire

<u>February 1951</u>

Jake Sorrells heard a car door slam. He set his chipped coffee cup down on the cable spool that served as a kitchen table. He crossed the few feet to where he kept his .45 Army Colt and slid it into the waistband of his jeans. Standing at the side of the door to the trailer house, he opened it a few inches. A late model sedan was parked at the mailbox, a heavyset man of sixty-something was checking the number on the box. Satisfied he had found the right address, he walked towards the trailer, his hands raised in the air.

Sorrells knew him. He set the Colt on the table before stepping out onto the porch. "How did you find me?" he asked.

Bob Philpot smiled. "That's what I do for a living. I find people," he said. "How are things, Jake?"

"Depends. What do you want?"

"If it's any comfort to you, Jake, tracking you down hasn't been easy. I've been looking for you for a month."

"Okay, so you found me. What's on your mind?"

"Nice place you got here," Philpot said surveying the shabby trailer.

"I rent it because it's cheap," Jake replied. "C'mon in, I've got coffee on."

"That would be good. I got something you may be interested in. A client requires a service that's way out of my line." Philpot pulled two one hundred dollar bills from his wallet and handed them to Sorrells.

"That's what it pays?"

"Hell no, that's just to show up. Call it expense money. You get the rest when the job's done."

"Sit down, Bob, you've got my attention."

Philpot looked at what passed as a chair, trying to decide if it would hold his weight. There were only two chairs at the table and Sorrells had threatened to throw one out. He didn't encourage guests. Jake filled the coffee cups and sat down across from Philpot. He reached for a pack of Lucky Strikes in his shirt pocket, lit one with an old army issue Zippo and leaned forward.

"My client is a widow lady," he began. "She lost her husband five years ago. They built a small asphalt company into a multi-state road construction business and made a lot of money in the process. She had one child, a boy who tried to take over when his father died. The kid began hanging out with the fast crowd up in Denver and got into big time gambling. Pretty soon he was way over his head. He had markers out to a bunch of tough characters. Finally, when they had him under water, they put the pressure on. These guys were leaning on him hard. Pretty soon he was using company money just to pay interest on his markers. That's when a guy named Marco DeVilla came to see him. DeVilla is a big time racketeer. Things like prostitution, drugs and loan sharking. The feds were always trying to bust him, but he was smart enough to buy the right people off and he was hiding the money in some shell companies he established that at least had the appearance of legit operations. A couple of them dealt in state contracts, the asphalt business was a natural, and again, he had the right connections. The kid agreed to help him set up contracts for materials that never came close to meeting minimum specs.

"My client, Mrs. Alcott, never knew the trouble the boy was in till an outside accounting firm found the discrepancies and told her. The accountants also found the fake invoices he had provided for DeVilla. When the accountants and Mrs. Alcott confronted her son, he broke down and told the whole story. As you can imagine, Mrs. Alcott was distraught, but told her son she would give him the money to pay off his debts. To his credit he refused, telling his mother he would handle the problem himself."

"How'd that work?" Sorrells interjected.

"They found the kid's body in a vat of hot oil they used to make asphalt. The coroner said he'd probably been alive when they threw him in the vat."

"Did your Mrs. Alcott go to the cops?"

"Many times," Philpot replied. "I went with her several times myself. All of them told her they were working on the murder and several other cases they had current on DeVilla, but that was all they would offer. That was a year ago and Mrs. Alcott has decided that nothing will be done and she wants her son's killers to pay for their crime."

Jake's head shook knowingly. He understood exactly what she wanted. "What does this Mrs. Alcott know about me?"

"Nothing except I recommended you, and that's the way I want to keep it."

"Me too," Jake nodded.

"Oh," Bob Philpot added, "she wants to meet you."

"Why? We just talked about her staying out of the problem."

"She wants to size you up, I suppose."

"Where does this meeting take place?"

There was a wide smile on his face when Philpot replied. "The Broadmoor."

"That's a pretty high class place."

"Yeah, but, Jake, this is a high class dame."

"When?"

"I'll have to call you."

"Hell, Bob, do you see a phone in here?"

"Saturday, a couple of days from now, I'll make it work out," Philpot said, "and Jake, get yourself some kind of sport coat and a tie. There are places in the Broadmoor you can't get in without a coat and tie. Take it out of the $200 and I'll call it expense money."

The Broadmoor, one of the best hotels West of the Mississippi River, was at least a two hour drive from Manassas. Jake Sorrell's only transportation was a dilapidated old pre-war Ford pickup. Jake didn't like to own anything he couldn't walk away from. The trip took him more than three hours and four quarts of oil. The old truck pulled into one of the Broadmoor's numerous parking areas in a cloud of smoke. Jake decided to park it as far away as possible from the hotel. He pulled the new Hart's blazer he'd bought on the road over his only dress shirt and put on the knit tie he'd bought at the same time and walked towards the hotel and the lady who wanted revenge for her only son's life.

Bob Philpot was waiting for him in a small lobby.

"You cleaned up pretty well, Jake," he grinned.

Jake made no response.

"I'll call and tell her you're here," Bob said, rising from a plush leather chair. "She tells me she'd prefer to see you alone."

"Okay."

Mrs. Alcott answered Jake's knock. "You are Mr. Sorrells?"

"Yes ma'am, Jake Sorrells."

"Please come in, Mr. Sorrells." Jake followed her into the sitting room of her suite. "May I get you a drink?"

"No ma'am, thank you."

"Do excuse me, but I think I will ... this conversation will be

THE GERMAN WOMAN'S HIRED HAND

difficult for me."

"I understand," Jake replied.

Mrs. Alcott was exactly as Sorrells had imagined. A stately, well-dressed woman of about sixty. She sat across from Sorrells and took a filter-tip cigarette from a silver box on a table next to her. Sorrells started to rise to light it for her but she already had a lighter in her hand.

"I understand Mr. Philpot has explained my reason for acquiring your services."

"He has," Sorrells replied. "I'm sorry for your loss."

Mrs. Alcott managed a polite smile.

"You need to know that I realize you want your son's killers to pay for what they did, but I am not an assassin. I do understand justice, and if I agree to take responsibility for providing you justice, someone will die."

"I do," she said softly.

"If I decide to take this job, you will leave the hotel as soon as possible and never contact me again. Mrs. Alcott, that is to protect you as much as me."

"I understand."

"Any future contact will be through Bob Philpot. You and I have never met."

She nodded.

Jake Sorrells continued. "My fee will be $2000 and expenses. Bob will handle the payment. Are these terms agreeable?"

"They are," she said. Her eyes were steely. "Mr. Sorrells, I want Marco DeVilla dead."

"Yes ma'am, I understand." Sorrells rose from his chair and took her offered hand and left to meet Bob Philpot in the lobby.

"Bob," said Sorrells, "tell me everything you know."

"For one thing, Jake, you won't have to do any looking. He's got a camp not far away. That's one reason I asked Mrs. Alcott to meet us here. And," he added, "this may be easier than you expect. Frankly, the cops will probably welcome DeVilla's demise and they will assume it's some sort of trade war between gangsters. Nobody would suspect a classy business woman or a war hero."

"Or at least not a dead one," Jake Sorrells said with only a trace of a smile.

Philpot reached into his brief case and produced a hand-drawn map and handed it to Sorrells. "That's a map of a hunting lodge DeVilla owns. Now let me tell you when he will be there. All his other interests aside, DeVilla's great love is gambling. Every few months he invites a group of his associates to the lodge for a three-day poker game. If he keeps to his schedule, the next poker game is this weekend. That should give you time to make a reconnaissance and determine a plan of action."

"You've done your job well, Bob. You've made it pretty damn simple for me, the trick will be getting out alive. Can you get me a room here at the hotel?"

"I've already done so, and one for me too, although I'd rather we not appear together. I've made our reservations under assumed names."

"There's one more thing, Bob," Jake said. "There's some things I'll need back at the trailer in Manassas. I'm not sure my truck is up to another three-hour trip; besides, if you'll drive me, we can go down and be back before ten tonight."

"It's done," Philpot said. "Let's go."

Jake Sorrells was proud of the fact he didn't have many possessions, only the resources he needed for his specialized occupation. The trailer court had a storage building located on its premises. After a brief stop at the trailer to pick up a few clothes, the final stop before returning to the Broadmoor was the storage building, where a series of locked bins lined one wall. Sorrells carried one key in his pocket. The key was to the storage bin. Inside, neatly stacked or attached to hooks on the walls were rifles, military and civilian pistols of several types, knives and several wooden boxes that contained explosive materials. He quickly chose what he might need, including wire cutters, a camouflage jacket and a pair of binoculars.

Philpot helped him load the items into the trunk of the car. Sorrells had loaded the last of his two boxes of explosives before he turned to Philpot. "Bob, if I were you, I'd drive real carefully and make damn sure you don't hit any big bumps." He ended his statement with a sly grin.

The next morning, Philpot drove Sorrells to the mountain location of DeVilla's hunting lodge. As he had suspected, the twenty acre property was surrounded by a six foot cyclone fence topped with barbed wire. It did not appear to be electrified. There was a formal gate and a gravel road that led to the lodge. All the property within sight was heavily wooded in pine timber. DeVilla's property was not too different from some other recreational locations in the area.

That evening, Sorrells gathered a few of his tools and drove back to the lodge. He parked his rented car a half mile away and walked to the DeVilla property. It was well after sundown and the moon was in crescent.

The road in front of the lodge was not heavily traveled, but Sorrells checked for car lights in each direction, then knelt beside the chain link fence and carefully cut the wires in such a manner that he could reconnect them later.

He crept through the pinewoods paralleling the gravel road to the lodge. All timber had been cleared around the lodge. There was a large barn-like structure behind the house that Sorrells assumed was used to store lawnmowers and other equipment. Two cars were parked in front of the house. He saw no one outside, so he assumed security was not a high priority.

Philpot had told him the big game would be that weekend if it kept to the normal schedule. Right or wrong, Sorrells believed that

Marco DeVilla was not currently in residence but probably would be the night before the game was scheduled in order to see that everything was prepared. Sorrells stayed for another forty-five minutes, but nothing noteworthy occurred. Tomorrow night he would return and bring the tools necessary to fulfill his commitment to Mrs. Alcott to avenge her son's death.

The following night he could make out a new Lincoln sedan parked immediately in front of the lodge's door and a man leaning against it smoking a cigarette. He was obviously standing watch. There were flood lights that lit only the front of the lodge. The rest of the property including the barn was in total darkness.

Sorrells had choices. He could bring down the lodge with one massive explosion or he could create a diversion. He chose the latter. He felt the situation called for a more personal solution. It was a simple plan. Sorrells felt no need to make it unduly complicated. Too many things could go wrong. He prepared the necessary devices in the dark of the woods. He had sufficient skills to have done so blindfolded. Then he moved through the darkness to place two separate bombs, which he set on a timer. One would detonate, and ten minutes later the second. Neither would bring down the barn, but they would certainly create loud explosions and the fire that resulted. That done, he crept back to the woods and carried his tools back to his parked rental car.

The next night Bob Philpot drove him to the hole he'd cut in the fence. Philpot asked him when to come back.

"Bob, if this thing goes as planned, you'll know. There will be two loud explosions. When you hear that, pick me up here." Sorrells carried his sniper rifle in one hand. In the other he held a canvas bag containing a detonator. In his belt was his Army issued .45. He knelt down to push the tools under the cyclone fence and then squeezed through it himself.

In his previous visits, Sorrells had determined the preferred location for his one-man attack on the lodge. He had cut a Y shaped branch for a tripod. He pushed the end of the branch into the damp soil, and after adjusting the rifle's scope, he pushed three shells into the clip and slid the breach open to chamber the only shell he would need.

Again tonight, only one man was stationed outside. Every light in the lodge was on. Somewhere inside, Marco DeVilla was no doubt relaxing before his guests arrived tomorrow night. It was early in the evening. Sorrells waited patiently. There was no need to rush. Once more he sighted his rifle and laid it across his handmade tripod. At a hundred yards, an easy shot. Bob Philpot had shown him pictures of DeVilla. He was a large man with a substantial belly. He would likely be the last man out of the lodge. Sorrells checked the time. His watch had one of those new radium dials that glowed in the dark. It was 8:13, although at this point, time was not a concern. He pulled the detonator towards him and depressed the switch that would ignite the first bomb, then waited till he heard the explosion. One side of the barn burst into flames. He watched as the occupants of the lodge rushed out to see what had happened. Some of them rushed towards the inferno. As he had thought, the large man he had recognized as DeVilla was not rushing anywhere.

Sorrells pushed the lever that produced the secondary explosion and lay down to make his shot. The fire had illuminated the whole scene. Sorrells gently squeezed the trigger and the big man jerked forward. "Mister DeVilla," Sorrells said aloud, "Mrs. Alcott wanted me to meet you." Then he gathered his tools and ran back to the road. As he had thought, Bob Philpot had no problem knowing when Sorrells had completed his work. The night sky was red with flames.

That same night, Sorrells loaded his tools into his old truck and drove back to Manassas with two thousand dollars cash inside his shirt. Three days later he had gone into a local beer joint and been involved in a fight with several toughs. Even drunk, he won easily. In the process, the police arrived and he'd fought them as well, and had spent the next five days in jail. A member of the local V.F.W. read his name in the paper and asked a member who was an attorney, to see what might be done to get him released. The lawyer had checked his military record, noted his previous medical problems and arranged for Sorrells to be transferred to the VA hospital in Denver.

Chapter Two
War Bride

Helga Marston pushed back the kitchen curtain and took in the rough beauty of the Western Oklahoma ranch land. The sparse serenity had brought her comfort from the first, a buffer against the sharp edges of her husband's nature. Thank God he was gone.

She folded the dishtowel and hung it over the oven door to dry, then stepped outside the kitchen door to throw cold dishwater onto her newly tilled garden plot. It was closing in on March. She had hoped the soil would loosen up before planting time, but the drought continued. A lesser woman might have given up hope that the northwestern Oklahoma sand could be persuaded to nurture growth of any kind, but she was not a lesser woman.

"Shoo!" she scolded the rooster scratching nearby, one shiny black eye on his busy harem. A wry smile nudged her lips. Has it come to this? she thought. Nurturing a garden and talking to chickens? Her life was unfolding far differently than she had imagined.

Five years ago, in the winter of 1946, Helga had left her mother in Berlin and crossed the Atlantic to marry Captain John Marston. She endured weeks of wild seas aboard the *USS McCallum* with other German war brides and fiancées, but her trials had just begun.

Sausage sizzled in the skillet, biscuits browned in the oven. Her two hired hands would expect their breakfast soon. How good it was to be rid of the big black iron wood burning stove that had been waiting for her when John brought her here to the ranch. Nothing was as she had pictured it. She shuddered as she stood at the kitchen window watching the sunrise.

How Helga had come to be in Oklahoma still seemed unreal. The war had ended. Berlin was in ruins and times were hard. Though Helga Heinke and her mother had a roof over their heads, their food, fuel and clothing were rationed. Every able-bodied person was required to go to work, or else the all-important ration-card would be denied.

When Helga's mother learned that the U.S. Army was looking for English-speaking help, she sent her daughter to apply. Because of the English that Helga had learned in school, she was hired, and that was how she came to work for Captain John Marston, manager of a newly opened PX.

She accepted his offer to drive her home after work one day, her mother opened the door to the handsome captain and her daughter, and their lives changed forever.

There had never been sympathy for Helga Heinke Marston in Dibs, Oklahoma, or, for that matter, in all of Woodson County. Too few years had passed since the war ended, and she had never been known as anything other than the German woman. Except for Melba McCrory, not even among the women who valued Helga's needlework and flaunted the tiny *hh* logo she embroidered in hidden corners.

Marston had effectively laid the groundwork for the locals' judgmental attitude toward his wife. He, a war veteran, was one of them, though a poor excuse for a rancher. He had sunk a fortune into the house and land out east of town, but the caliber of cattle he brought to market was far from standard. Still, the locals reasoned that it was a shame for any man to be saddled with a sullen, cantankerous woman.

Keeping up appearances was important to John Marston. Only his wife knew the cruel shell of a man he was, and he silenced her with threats she had reason to know he would fulfill. It had been easy to convince the German-hating post-war locals that, though his wife could speak English well, she refused to do so out of respect for her homeland. When asked why they never attended social events, he claimed she refused to mingle with what she termed "common folks."

Marston did allow his wife to attend an occasional service at the Lutheran church in Woodson thirty miles to the north, but only if she could get a ride.

Saturdays, he took her into town with him to do the grocery shopping. Afterwards, she waited for him throughout the afternoon at the local café while he exchanged war stories with his cronies at the stockyards. Helga was allowed only that one freedom among the Dibs residents, and how grateful she was for it. She would otherwise not have been invited into the back room of the cafe where Melba stored her mother's sewing machine.

Melba's interest lay in numbers and calculations, marketing and investments. Those who frequented the cafe would be surprised to know that Melba, their waitress, Clem McCord's daughter, had run a successful business in California.

Helga was very much interested in both the machine and the stacks of rich, colorful cloth, remnants that Melba's mother had accumulated over time. They filled the cafe storeroom to overflowing. When Helga first voiced her astonishment, Melba was surprised to learn that her little German friend was quite capable of speaking the language of her adopted land.

She spoke English so well, in fact, that over the next several Saturdays, the two of them laid out a plan involving the storeroom's treasures, a plan they hoped would profit the entire community.

Now that Marston was gone, many of the Dibs citizens believed his wife should give up the ranch and go back where she came from, but she had no family and no place to go. Her decision had been made for her when she married a man she didn't love and grew to detest.

Before her husband disappeared, a year of good rains had insured enough grass to produce a bumper calf crop that he sold at a fair price, but this year's drought had forced local producers to sell at whatever price could be had. Bank notes had been paid late or not at all, and Helga had been surprised to learn that her operating money was almost gone.

With hard times upon her, Helga resorted to operating the ranch short handed, and the two hands she had at that time were practically worthless. She fed them and housed them and paid what she could. One of them had bristled when his pay was short.

"You think you can do better elsewhere?" she countered. "Then go."

Both of the hands stayed on, but she often wished they hadn't. As likely as not, they disregarded her orders, preferring to lie around the bunkhouse between chores or hang out in town when she sent them on errands.

Except for Melba, Rev. Eli Steigner, pastor of Woodson's Lutheran Church and his wife, Mary, were her only friends. One Sunday when she asked him for advice regarding her hired help, the Reverend, a retired army chaplain, said he thought he knew someone who could help her in the short term. A man he had met in his previous service.

"He likes ranch life and he's dependable," the Reverend said. "I'll have to do some checking around. It's been several years since I've seen him."

Mary smiled her encouragement. "If anyone can help you," she said, "Eli can. Now come on home with us. I have a pot roast in the oven, and there's plenty to go around. Eli and I will drive you back to Dibs before evening services." Helga left that afternoon not knowing if Reverend Steigner could help her or not, but happy to have been with people who cared.

The Reverend began to fulfill his promise with a letter to Jonas Maclyn, a rancher in northern New Mexico, the last known employer of the man he needed to contact. He spelled out the nature of Helga's problem and her need for immediate help. "Someone who will stick it out to the end regardless of the difficulties," he wrote.

Two weeks later, he received a reply: "Dear Rev. Steigner, I have found Jake Sorrells. However, in his present state, I am afraid he will not be of much help to your friend. Sorrells was recently involved in a situation in Colorado that resulted in his arrest. When his military record was revealed, the court placed him in the care of the Denver VA hospital.

"It is my understanding that for the last three months he has been in their drug and alcohol recovery program. Even if the VA agrees to release him into your custody, I doubt Mrs. Marston's problem can be alleviated by a man with his particular skills. Nonetheless, I enclose the Denver VA address. Sincerely, and good luck, Jonas Maclyn."

Eli understood Maclyn's reservations, but no one knew Sorrells better than he did. Following an exchange of correspondence, the administrator of the VA hospital agreed to meet with Eli to discuss the possible release of the patient into his custody.

In the meantime, the hospital contacted the court where Sorrells' case originated, and the court expressed no desire to see him back in their jurisdiction. Specifically, the judge responded, "Do anything that fool preacher wants to do with him, as long as he does it in Oklahoma."

Reverend Steigner drove to Denver, signed the papers put before him, and set out for Dibs, Oklahoma, with Jake Sorrells sitting beside him.

"I think they figure they got the best of this deal," Sorrells said with a grin.

When the Reverend didn't answer, he added, "I need to pick up my truck and the rest of my gear in a town up the way. I rented a trailer. A guy I know said he'd keep an eye on things for me."

"A friend?" Steigner asked.

Sorrells smiled for the second time that day. "No, I guess not. Looks like I just got one of those."

Eli waited in the car while Jake moved numerous boxes and carefully wrapped bundles into the bed of his beat-up old pickup and tossed a saddle and some other tack along with a duffel bag into the cab. Then he reached behind a tattered sofa and pulled out a handful of cash, which he was sticking down his shirtfront when Eli spoke from the doorway.

"I thought you might need some help," he said, "but you appear to have handled it on your own. Is there anything I can do?"

"That's about it. Be right with you."

Sorrells found an old pair of cowboy boots, a hat and a corduroy coat, then shuffled through a stack of mail and pulled out three months' worth of VA disability checks, ignoring the rest, which were mostly bills.

Eli followed Jake to a corner filling station where he filled the tank, then walked over to put his hand on Eli Steigner's shoulder. "Let's go to Oklahoma," he said.

Chapter Three
Working Together

The next afternoon, two vehicles plowed up the dirt road to Helga Marston's ranch house, kicking up dust in all directions and setting the blackbirds to flight. As she stepped out onto the porch to greet her friend the Reverend, Helga saw the old pickup belching smoke behind him, steam spewing from the radiator. The Reverend stepped out of his car and walked toward the house as Sorrells emerged in degrees from his ramshackle truck, ground out the butt of his cigarette with the heel of his boot, stretched himself, and set out to join them.

Helga smiled up at the Reverend. "This is a pleasant surprise," she said. "What brings you here, and who is your friend?"

"Somebody I want you to meet," he replied with a grin, enjoying his little surprise. "Jake Sorrells, meet Helga Marston, your new boss. Treat her well. She's quite a lady." Then, turning to Helga, he added, "Sorrells will make you a good hand, Helga. Don't let the rough edges fool you."

When she offered her hand, Sorrell's grip was firm, but what Helga noticed even more were the pale gray, piercing eyes looking directly into her own.

"Could you tell me where you want me to store my gear?"

"There will be several empty cots in the bunkhouse," she said.

"I'll bring down clean towels and bed linens later. We have a storage room in the barn for anything you need to secure. Once you're finished, will you join Reverend Steigner and me back here at the house?"

Jake might have nodded, but Helga didn't think so.

He pulled the duffel bag from his truck and carried it into the bunkhouse where two men straddling a bunk played poker with a greasy deck of cards. Neither spoke. It was easy to identify the available bunks. They were the neat ones.

He dropped his duffel bag on the farthest one, unzipped it, and removed a clean white T-shirt. When he pulled his soiled shirt over his head, the two palmed their cards and looked at each other in disbelief. Sorrells tucked in his shirt and stuffed his soiled shirt into a bag he'd removed from the duffel. Then he shoved both bags under the bunk he had chosen and nodded in the general direction of the two hands as he left the bunkhouse.

"Shit!" one of them exploded. "Did you see that guy's chest? I ain't never seen so damn many scars."

In the ranch house kitchen, Reverend Steigner was preparing to enjoy a slice of his hostess's berry pie. "Well, Helga," he said "What do you think of your new hand?"

She busied herself cutting the pie she had made that morning and then took down cups for her guests. "I don't know yet," she finally said, "but you must think highly of him or you wouldn't have brought him here."

Eli appreciated her confidence. He chose his words carefully. "I do," he said. "I think he's exactly the man you need right now. But I must warn you, he's complicated, and he's got a history." He might have said more if there hadn't been a knock at the door. "Just trust me," he said hurriedly. "I know this is the right thing for both of you. Give him a chance."

Eli left and Sorrells asked his new employer to direct him to

THE GERMAN WOMAN'S HIRED HAND

the storage area she had mentioned earlier. "Does it have a lock?" he asked.

"No, but we can get one if you feel you need it."

"I think I've got what I need to secure the room. If you don't mind, that's what I'd like to do."

Sorrells returned to the bunkhouse, where the two hands were still throwing greasy cards down on the bunk between them.

"My name's Billy Maples," said the tall one. "This here is Joe Damron."

"I'm Sorrells. Jake Sorrells." There were wary handshakes all around. Wariness was Sorrells' nature. The hired hands were remembering the scars, eager to know the story, reluctant to ask.

"You signed on?" Damron asked.

"I'm signed on," Sorrells replied as he left for the storage room.

Maples and Damron went along to watch as he measured a section of chain, cut it to the proper length, then attached a strong Yale lock.

"This stuff you're going to put in here, it's that valuable?" Maples asked.

"I don't know how valuable it is, but it's all I own."

The next morning during breakfast around the big table in Helga's kitchen, Sorrells asked if a map of the property was available. She said she had seen one, but if it couldn't be found, one could be drawn.

"What you need a map for?" Damron asked.

"I figure I'll ride the property. Get a feel for how it lays."

Marston had accumulated a few horses, and Helga had continued to care for them after he left. The one Sorrells saddled hadn't been ridden in a while. He humped his back as if to test his rider's horsemanship, but he soon settled down and offered no more protest. Jake had carried a compass for years. Before leaving, he marked his location and checked the saddlebag for notepad and pencils.

The ranch was small by some standards, but it was well laid out with cross fences in poor repair dividing the pasture. He saw where hay crops had been baled the year before. There were ample ponds, though low now due to the drought. A good rain would cure that. These were flat lands, but at the far end of the property line were hills through which a small creek ran out for a hundred yards or so and then angled off to the southeast. Willows and small brush lined either side of the creek bed.

Before noon, he rode up one of the hills, dismounted and loosened the saddle girt so the horse could chomp grass. Sorrells hunkered down with his back to a tree trunk. He felt stiff. It had been a while since he'd straddled a horse. He took out the notepad and studied the notations he had made on the way out. The fence needed patching in several places, but that could be easily handled. Some of the pasture was over-grazed and needed to be rested. The cows had calves at their sides, and those calves would need to be worked soon.

As he sat there, he felt calm, peaceful. The way he felt only when he was out like this. It was the kind of feeling he needed to take his mind off a constant, overwhelming desire for alcohol. That was a big part of the reason he liked ranch work. That and the fact that you didn't have too much contact with people. Eli Steigner knew that. He had done him a favor bringing him here.

When Jake got back to the house that afternoon, Maples and Damron weren't around. He unsaddled the horse, rubbed him down and fed him a couple of scoops of oats. The windmill at the barn was not working, so he opened the storage room and took out his toolbox. By dinnertime, he had the windmill pumping water into the stock tank it served.

Helga stirred a pot of beans simmering on the stove. The cornbread would be browning by the time the men arrived. She shook her head. Something would have to be done about those two worthless hands, but what? She needed help, and it was too soon to know if Sorrells was going to work out.

Sorrells washed the grease from his hands and arms with lye soap from the bunkhouse, pulled on a clean shirt, and made a mental note to find out how Mrs. Marston wanted him to handle his laundry. Then he walked to the house for dinner.

Helga served meals around the large table in her kitchen. Maples and Damron were still not back, so the two sat at either end of the table. Since neither was much of a talker, conversation was mostly based on what Sorrells had observed on his ride around the ranch. At one point, she asked him how he had come to know Eli Steigner.

"It was during the war. He was the chaplain at a hospital I was in for a while."

"He seems to think highly of you," she said.

"He's never judged me." Sorrells' shook his head and changed the subject. "Mrs. Marston, there's things that need doing around here, but I don't see much help coming out'a Maples and Damron. Is there a reason for that?"

"I know," she said, looking down at the table. "They were all I had, but I know I've got to do something about them. I've just put it off."

"I'm not trying to run your business, ma'am, but would you want me to have a talk with them?"

That night Maples and Damron burst into the bunkhouse, rowdy and smelling of alcohol. They paid no attention to Sorrells, who lay on his cot with his back to them. The smell of alcohol was even more maddening to Jake than the noise that had waked him. He was soon on the edge of his bunk, then on his feet and moving purposefully toward the two men.

"Don't either of you ever come around me like this again!" he barked. "You need to hit your bunks now. We got a busy day tomorrow."

Damron started to respond but changed his mind.

"I'll ... I'll see you in the mornin'," Maples said, and they did. Jake rousted them out of their bunks long before dawn.

"Hell, it ain't light yet!" Damron complained.

Sorrells showed them places he had marked on his map where the fences needed patching. "Take some tools and get started," he ordered.

"What about breakfast?" one of them whined. "Don't we get to eat?"

"You can come in at seven. Maybe you'll have worked up an appetite by then."

Damron started toward him, his back bowed. "Who made you the damn boss? We ain't work'n for you!"

"You're not working at all," he said. "That's the problem, but things have just changed. You're going to earn your keep or get off the place. I may put you off anyway. Now get started."

Two days later, Jake took money from his pocket and paid them off.

"What will we do?" asked Helga. "I know they were no good, but now we don't have anybody for the work."

"Like I said, Mrs. Marston, that's just the point. They weren't working. Now at least you won't be paying them for nothing. I'm sorry if I've done something you don't like, but to me, a man needs to earn his pay."

"You're right, of course, Mr. Sorrells. We'll manage. I'll work beside you."

The next day, Helga pulled on leather gloves and a pair of her husband's old jeans and helped Sorrells make the necessary fence repairs. By the time they got back to the house that late afternoon, her fair skin was burned a blistering red and her arms had been cut by barbed wire. She was tired, but she had done well and knew it.

That evening, Sorrells helped with the sandwiches they ate for supper, but Helga had trouble keeping her head off the table long enough to eat them. "I'll clean up in the morning," she said as she crippled off to bed. "Just ... just turn off the light and lock the door when you leave."

The next day before they returned to finish the job, she wrapped her long braids about her head and pulled one of her husband's hats down low on her forehead.

Chapter Four
Mason's Feed Store

One of the first things Sorrells had noticed as he toured the Marston land the day after he arrived was that the grassland was over grazed. Toward the end of his third week on the Marston place, he announced his plans to go into town and buy enough feed to tide the mother cows over.

Helga said she needed to buy groceries and would ride in with him. She believed she had enough cash to handle that. If not, surely her credit would hold up at least one more time at the feed store. The dress she wore was one of her own creations, cut modestly, but anyone could see that it fit. The skirt swished around her bare legs as her sandaled feet carried her to the truck where Sorrells waited.

Helga's recently fired hands, Maples and Damron, had spent most of their time and all of the money Sorrells had paid them at the town's beer joint. When their drinking buddies tired of hearing the already embellished story of how they came to leave the Marston place, they took their story to new heights.

"That new hand – Sorrells, he calls hisself – he come in and started throwin' his weight around, orderin' us to do more than any man ought to have to do. Workin' us way before dawn and without breakfast. That there German woman, she's doin' whatever he says. If you ask me, them two has got somethin' goin' on, if you know what

I mean. Truth is, we seen 'em."

The locals were prepared to believe anything was possible as far as the German woman was concerned. "That's what you can expect from them foreigners," they said among themselves. "Them Nazis don't know the meaning of decent. It's no wonder that Yankee husband of hers run off. Course, he shouldn't never have brought her over here in the first place."

Long before Sorrells and Helga drove into Dibs that day, the fired hands' stories had been heard and believed by all, including Ed Mason, the owner of the feed store. Mason spent little time at his store these days. For the last couple of years, he had left for lunch at the café, after which he played dominoes and swilled beer with his buddies at the pool hall until mid-afternoon.

He was returning to the store as Sorrells was parking the truck out front. One too many beers, coupled with his hatred for all things German, raged through him when he saw the German woman and that boyfriend of hers stopped in front of his store.

The feed store was an afternoon hangout for friends of Mason's two burly sons, Sid and Fred. This day, two or three of those friends were sitting inside on stacks of feed sacks rehashing Friday night's high school football game when Helga entered the store with Sorrells behind her. Sid, the older of Mason's boys, leaned against the counter watching appreciatively as she approached and laid a list of her needs on the counter.

"I'll have to check this out with my dad," he said. Just then, Ed Mason pushed open the door hard enough to bang as it slammed against the wall.

"Hold on, son," he said, loud enough for everyone to hear. "We ain't running no charity here!"

Helga's anger flared, but her voice was level when she said, "Mr. Mason, I'm not asking for charity. My credit has always been good and you have profited from the business the Marston Ranch has brought you these past years. I have always paid by the month and I will at the end of this month as well."

Ed was feeling the effects of his two-hour beer drinking bout and he had an audience to entertain. "I see you can speak English after all," he snarled, "but you sure as hell don't understand it. I don't want your damn business. Never have. Not now. Not ever. You and your boyfriend get out'a my store!"

Helga's sunburned face paled and her body stiffened. Jake took her arm and led her outside to the truck. "Wait here," he said.

He interrupted a good laugh when he stepped back through the door, but a hush fell over the place as he walked to the counter and picked up the list Helga had left. "Fill the lady's order," he said.

Ed's reputation was at stake. He ripped the list from Jake's hand and crushed it in his fist. "I told you and that German bitch. ..."

Sorrells hadn't intended to start with the father. The boys had grown to manhood lifting hundred pound sacks of grain, the old man was fifty at least and reeking of beer. But the decision was made for him when the senior Mason threw the first punch and ended up face down on the floor. Then Jake turned to face his sons.

Afterwards, the witnesses all told the same story: Mason was out cold, but his boys put up a hell of a fight. Fred grabbed Sorrells while Sid hit him, and he should have gone down, but didn't. It was finished as suddenly as it had begun. Sorrells leaned against the counter, bent over due to blows to his body, his face covered in blood. The Mason boys sprawled on the floor beside their father. Their friends told each other later they were thinking about moving in themselves when Sorrells' held his arm out palm forward and said, "Don't even think about it."

When it appeared the excitement was over, Sorrells knelt over the older of the fallen brothers. "The list," he said. "It'll be on the floor beside your daddy. Get it. Fill Mrs. Marston's order and we'll be going. She'll be paying cash."

Helga sat rigidly in the truck as the revived Mason boys piled sacks of feed onto the truck bed. Sorrells reached inside his torn shirt and handed Sid Mason what she owed, then sent him inside to write a receipt. Ed staggered out with it, yelling, "I don't want your damn business!"

"Yeah?" Sorrells replied, "well, like it or not, this time you got it."

Several citizens gathered on the sidewalk to watch as Jake painfully pulled himself up into the truck. As he started the engine, he turned to Helga and said, "I hope things go smoother at the grocery store." He tried to smile, but his lips wouldn't move that much.

"We'll leave that for another day," she replied as she opened her door, then walked around the truck and opened his. "Move over," she said. "I'm driving."

The sacks of feed stayed on the truck that night, and Helga helped Sorrells into the house. His ribs had been badly bruised, if not cracked, and he couldn't straighten the upper part of his body. When she unbuttoned his torn shirt, the cash he carried there fell to the floor. Without a word, she gathered the scattered bills and placed them on the table beside him.

"I saw where the money came from when you paid Ed Mason," she said. "It's a loan, not a gift."

Sorrells nodded.

She washed the blood from his face and medicated the open wounds. While removing what was left of his shirt, she noticed without comment a small tattoo of a parachutist on his shoulder. She rinsed the cloth in warm water and was washing away splatters of blood when her fingers brushed across the scars on his chest, and she froze. Anticipating her question, Sorrells said, "The war."

"Against the Germans?"

"Against the Germans," he said, then added, "in France."

She rubbed salve on his bruised lips and cheeks, then wrapped strips of cloth about his chest to stabilize his ribs. When he refused to lie down, she brought the feather pillows from her bed and placed them between his torso and the arms of the chair where he sat.

"Thanks," he said, unused to the attention but grateful for her care.

Neither of them could eat, so they settled for coffee and sat in silence, immersed in private thoughts until well past sunset when Sorrells broke the silence bluntly. "What happened to your husband?"

Helga shrugged. "I don't know. He could be anywhere."

"What brought him here to Oklahoma?"

"Any out of the way place would have done. After he left Germany, in the month or so before I followed him here, he became involved with a young married woman, the daughter of a friend of his family back east."

"He told you that?"

"No, I came upon her letters after John left. His family gave him his inheritance shortly before I arrived, but with strings attached."

"What kind of strings?"

"He must marry immediately and move far away where he would no longer be an embarrassment to them. And so we married. This is the ranch he bought with his inheritance."

"What about your people?"

"Only my mother and I survived the war."

"And what became of her?"

"She killed herself soon after I left. John brought me the note she had written and mailed before she died. It was written in German *'Bitte verzeihen Sie mir!* Please forgive me.' Just that one line. John made me interpret it, but I told him she'd written, 'Get out while you can.' It would have been worth the beating if I hadn't lost the baby."

Helga hadn't known she was crying until Sorrells edged forward and wiped the tears from her face. She raised her eyes to meet his and found them strangely soft.

"I'd best be getting on out to my bunk," he said. "The pain's easing up some and you need your rest." He crossed the distance to the bunkhouse puzzling over the mystery that was Helga Marston.

Chapter Five
Dibs Sale Barn

The drought had officially broken by mid-June, and still the rain came down. Creeks filled to overflowing, and plowed fields became sucking bogs. Throughout the better part of late summer and early fall, life on the ranch was a curious mixture of jobs postponed by the welcome rains and emergency repairs due to those same rains.

One of those emergencies was discovered when Sorrells went out to check on a water guard crossing a creek that ran off the ranch property. He had chosen to saddle a horse, not trusting his old truck to keep from becoming stuck in the mud. He tied a slicker behind his saddle and rode to the creek, a distance of about half a mile. The rain had stopped as he'd ridden off from the barn, but the clouds were heavy and dark. Halfway to his destination, the clouds opened up and he found himself in nearly blinding rain. He had thought for a minute of returning to the barn, but he was too stubborn to give in to even nature's fury.

His decision to go on was proven to be the right one when, on arrival at the creek, he discovered a four hundred pound calf which had either wandered into or fallen into the creek and become stuck in the sucking mud beneath the water. The calf had fought to free himself but his efforts had left him exhausted, his head barely above the rapidly rising water.

Freeing the calf was not a job for one man and Sorrells was alone. Still, he took his lariat rope from the saddle and waded into the rushing water. He managed to secure the rope around the calf's forequarters, then crawled back to the bank to tie the rope to his saddle horn. The cowhorse knew what he was expected to do and slowly moved backwards, eventually pulling the calf to safety. They were both too exhausted to stand, but somehow Sorrells found the spectacle amusing. They were both drenching wet and covered in mud, but the calf would need to be returned to the herd. He knelt beside the calf, untied the rope and sat there laughing at their combined awkwardness till the animal was finally able to stand.

If Sorrells had ever needed a drink, it should have been then. Absent whiskey, however, he contented himself with knowing that all he and the calf had been through was simply a part of nature. That either life or death had been a possibility and he had done what it took for both of them to survive. Sorrells understood survival better than most men ever would.

Time never dragged around the Marston ranch, so Sorrells was surprised to one day realize that weeks had passed; the ranch-running funds were low; the operation was in need of supplies, and — assuming the whole of Dibs was of the same opinion that Ed Mason had made clear at the feed store — Mrs. Marston's credit line had apparently stopped.

Either way, the episode at the feed store had clearly established the necessity to raise cash for day-by-day operations, and Helga also had household needs. It was time for Sorrells to approach Mrs. Marston with a possible solution to their problem.

"You've got steers that are close to five hundred pounds," he told Helga at supper that night. "That's really not enough. They need to be at least six hundred or so, but why don't you let me cut out some of the culls and maybe we could come up with fifteen or twenty we could sell in town. I figure we could kill two birds with one stone — raise some quick cash and sell stock that we need to get rid of anyway."

To Helga, that seemed like a good solution. Certainly preferable to what had happened at the feed store. That had been a horrible embarrassment. "Mr. Sorrells, we are agreed," she said. "You will determine which steers to sell?"

"Yes, ma'am, I'll get right on it."

It took almost a week before the steers could be cut out and moved to holding pens up by the big barn. It took another week till the next sale date came around. During that time, the steers needed to be fed and watered in order to keep them from losing weight.

On the date of the sale, Sorrells and Helga managed to load the steers into the flatbed truck and he drove them to the sale barn in Dibs.

Jake backed the truck up to a loading ramp, raised the tailgate, and offloaded the steers into a narrow lane that separated a series of holding pens. He had stepped onto the ramp and started to push the steers forward when Les Jones, the sale barn's foreman, took over.

"This here your stock?" he asked.

"Marston Ranch," Jake replied.

"Get these here down to pen #6," he called out to the boy who did odd jobs on sale days. He hurriedly scribbled a receipt, tore it from his clipboard and handed it to Sorrells. "Take this to the office," he barked. "You'll have some papers to sign."

Jake was leaving when he heard the boy cry out and turned to see him wedged against the board railing. Jones was striking him with a stock whip.

"Please, Mr. Jones," he pleaded, "I didn't mean to. ..." The boy had not opened the gate to pen #6 and the Marston steers had pushed on past, blocking the lane.

Jake was no more than twenty feet away. Quarters were close, just the width of the lane, but in a matter of seconds, he had grabbed the foreman's arm. Jones was a big man and not accustomed to being challenged. He made a clumsy swing of the whip, which Sorrells easily avoided before raising both hands, palm forward. "I don't want any trouble," he said.

Apparently Jones did. Later, those of his friends who witnessed the scrap claimed not to have seen a blow struck on either side.

One said, "Jones was down in the mud and cow shit with that new guy's knee across his throat."

Another said, "The son'a bitch pulled Jones' head up by the hair and said something I didn't hear."

"I heard," claimed another: "'Don't ever touch that boy again or so help me, I'll kill you!'"

After it was over, Jake told the boy to leave the pen. "I'll see you in a minute," he said, and then he headed for the office.

"These steers belong to the German woman?" Smithers, the office manager asked.

"If you mean Mrs. Marston, yes, they're Marston stock."

"If they sell, tell her we'll mail her a check." Smithers turned to thumb through files at the side of his desk.

"They'll sell," Sorrells said, turning to leave, "I'll come back for the check later."

"You that guy who had the run-in at the feed store the other day?" Smithers asked as Sorrells turned to leave.

Sorrells heard but made no reply as he stepped out the door. The boy was waiting beside the truck.

"Thanks, mister. I'm sorry I caused you trouble," he said.

"You didn't," clipped Sorrells. "Do you work here?"

"Yes sir. Part time when they let me."

He folded the receipt for the steers and put it in his shirt pocket. "You need to get yourself something else to do. Your boss isn't likely to take what happened lightly."

"They say you're the new hand out at the German woman's place."

"Her name's Mrs. Marston, and yes, I'm the new hand."

"No offence intended. You reckon Mrs. Marston would let me sign on? I need the work."

"What's your name, son, and how old are you?"

"Charlie. Charlie Conn's my name and I'm fifteen."

"Well, Charlie Conn, what do you think your folks would have to say about that?"

"I don't rightly know. They ain't been around for a while."

"Get in the truck, Charlie. I've got some things to do while I'm in town. Then we'll come back here for Mrs. Marston's check."

"You ain't figuring to go back to the feed store anytime soon, are you?" Charlie asked.

"You heard about that?"

"Yes sir. Ever'body in the county has."

Chapter Six
Charlie Conn

Every eye in Clem's Café was on Sorrells when he walked in with Charlie shortly after one o'clock. The regulars had finished lunch and returned to work.

Melba tossed a lock of hair from her eyes and carried two glasses of water to the booth. "Hi Charlie," she said.

Charlie grinned, proud of the company he kept. "Hi Melba," he replied.

The town's only café offered no daily specials and no menus. A yellowing sign over the counter had listed the same offerings since the doors opened fifteen years ago. Locals joked that only the prices had changed.

"Hamburger and fries, Melba, and a coke."

"I'll have the same," said Sorrells, "but make mine coffee."

Melba called out their order to Clem in the kitchen, who echoed it for confirmation. He dropped a couple of handfuls of the potatoes he'd peeled and sliced that morning into a wire basket and lowered it into the hot oil. Then he slapped generous mounds of ground beef onto the sizzling grill and flattened them with a spatula.

Clem McCord was Melba's father. He was past the age when most would have retired, but he often joked that he was still the best fry cook in town. He laughed with the others when they reminded him that he was the only fry cook in town.

Melba and her girlfriend, Sadie Dale, had left Dibs the night of their high school graduation in the mid-thirties, Sadie to escape an abusive family situation and Melba to escape the howling Dust Bowl winds.

When Melba returned for her mother's funeral five years later, she found the familiar winds generally pleasant and mostly dust free. Her dad was eager for her to stay, and Melba came to a quick decision. She whipped off a letter to Sadie — who was known in the West Coast fashion world as Clarissa Fontaine — and settled down with her dad in the bungalow she had grown up in behind the café.

California had been good to Melba financially, but after the Japanese bombed Pearl Harbor, the coastline blackouts and the occasional scream of an air raid siren were unsettling. Besides, her long-term romantic involvement had exploded in her face and come close to destroying her too. She gratefully fell back into her small town life and had even come close to marrying once.

Thank God she learned what she needed to know about Les Jones before it was too late. Thirty-five wasn't all that old, and she might yet one day marry, but it wouldn't be to a man like that. She and Roy Strange, the town deputy, had been keeping company more frequently of late, and Melba had grown more than a little fond of her old high school chum. Roy was a man of few words, but she suspected the feeling was mutual.

When the food arrived, Charlie smothered his fries in catsup and they both attacked their hamburgers with pleasure enough to assure Clem that he was indeed the best fry cook in town.

"Can I ask you a question?" Charlie said between bites.

"That depends. What kind of question?"

"Where did you learn to fight like you do?"

Sorrells looked over the top of his hamburger at Charlie. "I was in the war. The army trains you."

The boy finished his burger and was working on the last of his fries before either of them spoke again. "There's lots of guys around here that was in the war," Charlie said. "Folks that saw you down at the feed story, some of them was in the war. They're tellin' that they never seen anything like you."

Jake motioned to Melba to bring the check. Instead, she rested a hand on the edge of the table and reached over to muss Charlie's hair. "You're a good kid, Charlie Conn. That damn Les had no call to treat you like he did." Sorrells' glance met hers and she said, "It's on the house, honey."

Jake smiled and nodded. When Melba walked away, he laid a five-dollar bill on the table.

"Tell Helga her sewing machine's still sittin' here in the back of the café when she's ready for it," Melba said as they were leaving, and tell her I got that letter we've been waitin' on. She'd have known that by now if she'd turn loose and get herself a telephone."

As the two walked back to the truck, Sorrells said, "Charlie, you just might be lucky. You still want to ask Mrs. Marston for that job?"

For several weeks, Charlie had been sleeping in one of the barns at the sale grounds. While Sorrells went into the office to collect the money for the steers, Charlie went to fetch his belongings.

When Sorrells walked out of the office, Charlie was waiting, paper sack under his arm. "Those your things?" Sorrells asked.

"All I got."

"Believe me, I understand."

"Do you reck'n they'd pay me what I got coming?" Charlie said with a motion toward the office door.

"They owe you money?"

"Yeah, some."

"We'll go ask. The worst they can do is say no."

Charlie opened the door and stepped over to the desk where the office manager sat thumbing through sales receipts. When Charlie asked about his pay, the office manager started to laugh, then looked up to see Sorrells standing behind the boy. He took a ten-dollar bill from the cash drawer and handed it to Charlie.

"That was easier than I figured," Charlie said.

"Yeah, easier," Jake replied.

When the truck turned back toward the café, Charlie thought he knew why. "We're gonna pick up Mrs. Marston's sewing machine?"

"Yeah. Might as well."

The sun was easing toward the horizon behind them when they headed back to the Marston place. Helga looked beyond the flapping laundry she was removing from the backyard clothesline and saw the cloud of dust rising. That would be Mr. Sorrells, she thought. Hopefully, with some money.

From her homeland, Helga had brought a talent for fine needlework. At first that talent afforded her a little independence. Now, with her husband gone, she relied on it to boost her modest income. Helga's inventory of saleable handwork was sure to increase many times over with the aid of a sewing machine.

Melba had insisted she take the old treadle machine with her last summer, but Helga hadn't made the final payment. She wouldn't be beholden to anyone, ever. Certainly not to one of the only friends she had on this side of the ocean.

She continued to unclip clothes pins and stash them in her apron, folding the dry sheets and towels right off the line and stacking them neatly, monotonously, in the basket at her feet. All the while, her thoughts were on the cattle truck lumbering toward her. She was eager to know how much her cattle had brought and if the driver of the approaching truck considered the amount to be fair.

Helga had reached the screen door, her basket of folded clothes balanced on a hip, when the truck drew even and a freckled face grinned at her from the passenger window. Her heart turned over and the basket slipped to the ground, scattering sheets and towels

THE GERMAN WOMAN'S HIRED HAND

in the sand.

That face! Her knees trembled and she braced herself, clinging to the doorframe as the setting sun evolved in her mind's eye into an inferno of leaping flames. The stench of burning flesh filled her nostrils, the crush and heave of crumbling stone walls filled her ears. Before the anguished cries faded from her memory, she slid to a sitting position in the doorway, fighting the urge to rush forward and search through the phantom rubble.

Charlie's wide-open freckled face was so very like little Hans', the brother she had lost in the Berlin bombing. Helga strove to shake the image of Hans' broken body from her mind. The pain of loss was too great. She would never allow herself to love that much again.

She dashed the tears from her eyes and was gathering up the scattered laundry when she saw what Sorrells and the boy were unloading from the truck bed. "This is Charlie," said Sorrells over his shoulder. "He thought he might make you a hand. Charlie, say hello to Mrs. Marston."

Swallowing hard, she stood up to hold the door open, and then she directed Sorrells to carry the sewing machine into her bedroom and place it beneath the north windows.

"Oh, my," was all she could manage. "Oh, my, oh, my."

"Got a good price on the cattle," Sorrells said. Charlie looked away. He had seen the final payment emerge from inside Jake's shirt before he went into the café and returned with the sewing machine.

Helga yearned to examine it more closely, but there would be time for that later. The talk around the table that evening concerned Charlie Conn's future. He sat quietly listening as they spoke of him as though he weren't there.

"I know we will need help, Mr. Sorrells, but he's just a boy," Helga said.

"Yes ma'am, he is, but I can teach him what he needs to know."

Charlie scuffed his boot against the chair leg while he waited for his fate to be determined.

"I don't know," she said. "He should be in school." She looked at Charlie, then rose to clear the table.

"Yes ma'am, but he isn't. Mrs. Marston, he needs a job. He's on his own, just like you."

"Oh, very well, we'll give you a trial, Charlie." Helga turned away to hide the smile that threatened to show itself. Hans would have been about Charlie's age if he had lived. It would be good to have young life around the place. "But you must work hard and do as Mr. Sorrells and I tell you. Do you understand?"

"Yes ma'am." Charlie smiled broadly. "I'll try real hard to make you a hand."

Helga watched from the window as the two of them put the cattle truck away, then proceeded on to the bunkhouse that would be Charlie's new home. She hadn't felt more complete in years.

Chapter Seven
Rusty Old Truck

It had taken the better part of a week, but the calves had been worked, and a good part of that had been done with a lariat and hard labor. At first Jake carried the bulk of the physical responsibility, but Charlie learned day by day what needed to be done and, being young, had grown eager to prove himself.

Helga had at first been repulsed by the castration and the branding, but it wasn't long before she pulled on heavy leather gloves to protect her hands and was heating the iron and stamping the MR brand on the hip of each bellowing calf.

When the last calf was released to return to its mother, Sorrells rose from his knees and looked around at his crew. Charlie beamed as he rolled up his lariat, apparently unfazed by the work and proud that he had made a hand. Helga, a hat pulled down almost over her eyes, her braids loose and falling down her back, remained bent over, her hands on her knees, catching her breath. Her face was dirty, but her lips wore the hint of a smile.

The three of them washed their hands and faces at the windmill trough, then Helga limped back to the ranch house. Charlie and Sorrells proceeded on to the bunkhouse. Later, after baths in the trough, they joined her in the kitchen for lemonade. "I'm proud of you," Sorrells told them. "I believe we've all earned a day off."

The next morning, Sorrells dressed quietly and left Charlie asleep in his bunk when he went to the storeroom to get his toolbox. His old pickup hadn't been started since the week before when Helga returned from Woodson with the vet supplies. He knew from long experience that it wouldn't start today. Sure enough, there was no sound as he turned the key and pushed the starter. He might as well use the day to go to town and see if he could find a new battery. He didn't know why he had put up with the old truck so long. There was enough money to buy something better. Ever since he was released from the hospital after the war, he hadn't placed much store in owning things. The simpler the better, he believed.

He raised the hood and was making a mental note of what might be needed to get the Ford in good running condition, when something brushed his shoulder. He turned to see that Charlie had crowded in under the hood beside him.

"You need any help?" he asked.

"You a mechanic?"

"You can teach me, I reck'n."

After lunch, they took the flatbed truck into Dibs for parts, and every evening after that, they worked on the pickup. Finally, after several more trips to town, they had it running. The radiator had been welded and hoses replaced. Sorrells pulled the heads and showed Charlie how to replace the old gaskets and plugs. He was always surprised at how fast the boy learned and how much he wanted to please. Jake wasn't one to waste time on compliments, but he made an exception with Charlie. He seemed to need all the attention he could give him.

Evenings after chores, Charlie took to sitting alone in the pickup, his hands on the wheel, his feet on the pedals, his mind racing until Helga called him for supper. Sorrells saw him there and was reminded that he had done the same thing.

"Charlie? You drive?" he asked.

"No sir, I reck'n not. I sure want to though."

"Well then, I guess I better teach you." Sorrells noticed again that it took very little to spread a grin across the face of the boy who might have been himself at that age.

As it would for most fifteen-year-old boys, driving even a beat up old pickup became the most important thing in Charlie Conn's life. Sorrells drove him out into one of the pastures and taught him to operate the three-speed transmission. Terrifying sounds of grinding metal put hundreds of field crows to flight before he learned to depress the clutch in conjunction with shifting the gears. The truck somehow survived, and Charlie became a passable driver.

It would be the better part of a year before he could apply for his drivers license, but in a rural area like this, kids commonly drove without observing that formality. Now when they rode together, it was Charlie behind the wheel. There was little paint left on the old truck, but no chariot ever looked better. Charlie washed it at least once a week.

Chapter Eight
New Addition

Sorrells felt himself falling through air. Flashes of light rose up from the ground. Something was horribly wrong. His parachute clipped a tree, snagged, and somehow managed to free itself, allowing him to fall to the ground.

He rose quickly and rolled up the chute as he had done a hundred times in training. Men shouted and gunfire flashed. He adjusted his heavy pack, slung the M1 Garand over his shoulder and, carrying his chute, ran into the woods.

Sweat-soaked and trembling, Sorrells woke to find himself sitting on the edge of his bunk. Charlie slept on, undisturbed by the horror that had jolted Jake awake. He sat there awhile longer, waiting for his heartbeat to slow down. That wasn't too bad, he told himself. I've had a lot worse. He lay back on the bunk and was soon lost in fitful sleep.

The next morning, he and Charlie saddled a couple of horses and rode off to check on the calves that had been worked a week ago. They were back at the ranch house by seven for breakfast, then out again to finish their inspection.

Sorrells generally didn't enjoy the company of others, yet there was something about the innocence of this boy that made him feel better about himself. Charlie wanted to please him. He worked hard and he learned. The boy looked up to Jake, and that bothered him. He knew he was a damn poor role model.

They got back to the barn in mid-afternoon, having found that, in general, the calves were all in good shape. They had roped one or two that required attention, applied the necessary medication, then turned them loose to return to their mothers. It was looking like rain, and that was good. If it didn't rain this time of year, the feed grass wouldn't grow and the ponds wouldn't fill up before summer.

Charlie's friends were already back in school, where he intended to join them this time next year. Helga had been working with him on his reading and writing Sunday afternoons and maybe half an hour each evening. He much preferred shadowing Sorrells, but he was attentive, and Helga was proud of his progress. With luck, he would be able to keep up with the other tenth graders next fall.

In the meantime, Charlie needed clothes. The few things he had brought in his sack were already worn out when he came to the ranch, and the boy was growing. Helga's cooking had a lot to do with that. At supper that night, Sorrells mentioned that he might take Charlie to town and get him a couple of shirts and some jeans.

Helga shook her head. "You needn't do that, Mr. Sorrells. Charlie is my responsibility. You don't have to spend your money."

They were doing it again. Charlie wished they wouldn't talk about him as though he wasn't in the room.

"Well, Mrs. Marston, I don't have much else to do with what little money I have. Spending some of it on Charlie here is as good as anything," said Jake.

"All right then, but no shirts. I will make shirts for Charlie myself, but only two. He'll outgrow them in no time, and I imagine he'd prefer T-shirts for everyday anyway. I'll go with you and he can choose the fabric, but I need to get his measurements. Bring me the tape measure, Charlie. It's on the sewing machine in my bedroom."

Charlie was grinning from ear to ear as he left the room, but his eyes were big when he returned. He hardly noticed that Helga was measuring him for pattern size. His mind was filled with visions of the dozens of brightly colored patchwork jackets hanging on a rod stretched the length of Mrs. Marston's bedroom. Must have something to do with the clacking noise he'd been hearing at night out in the bunkhouse where he and Sorrells slept. Sure are pretty, he thought, but who'd wear one of 'em?

Sorrells dropped Charlie and Helga off at McArthur's Mercantile, intending to wait out their shopping spree at the café, where Melba was in danger of losing the day's profit while making good on her five-cent coffee and free refills. The last of the breakfast bunch had left and the noon rush was still an hour away. She filled her cup and slid into the booth beside him.

"I see things are shaping up out at the ranch," she said. "Marston had big ideas, but he was all blow and no go. Thank God Helga's shut of him. For good, I hope."

"Charlie's good help," he said. "They've both got gumption."

"Helga wouldn't be alive today if she didn't. What that man did to her was a crime. A punishable crime, but no one knew about it except me till after he was long gone."

"You mean the baby she lost?"

"You know about that, do you? Good. I'm glad she can talk about it now. The baby would have been almost three years old if he had lived. No telling how many times she tried to run away after that. Got as far as the railroad track before he caught her the last time."

"Caught her?"

"He came at her on horseback out of the blackjacks. Herded her back to the house like you would a balky cow and tied her to the bed."

"She told you that?"

"I dropped off a cake a couple of days later. When no one answered my knock, I went on in and put it on the kitchen counter.

That's when I heard her moan. She'd been tied to that bed long enough for the bruises to start turning green."

"And Marston?"

"He was long gone by then. That was all that mattered to her. She wouldn't let me tell anyone, and I haven't until now. Helga was afraid of the law. Her dad died in prison, you know. The Nazis took exception to the anti-Hitler pamphlets he wrote."

Sorrells' thoughts swirled. So many conflicting emotions. So many unanswered questions. What he needed was a lung full of fresh air. Clem's Café was filling up. It was time to check on progress down at the mercantile.

He dropped a dollar on the table and nodded his goodbye. Melba waved. "Tell Helga I'll be out your way early tomorrow morning. See you then."

Wednesday was Melba's day off. For several weeks now, she had spent that day at the Marston ranch. The two women would have bits and pieces of shiny material strung out all over the house, and the clack-clack of the treadle sewing machine wouldn't stop till the sun went down. Jake and Charlie never suffered. Melba brought her daddy's famous barbecue and trimmings for lunch, and there would be stew and cornbread for supper. As if by magic, the house would be back in order by then.

Last Wednesday was different. A big shiny red Cadillac was parked beside Melba's car when Sorrells and Charlie returned to the house for lunch. The stranger's car bore a California license plate, but the black-haired, high-heeled lady sitting at the table was putting on no airs. She licked barbecue sauce off the diamond-studded fingers of one hand and reached for another rib with the other.

"Come on in and sit down, honey. Melba brought extra. I'll be out of your way soon as I finish this rib and we sign us some papers."

Clarissa Fontaine was as good as her word. The big red Cadillac kicked up a spray of sand as high as Charlie's head and then she was gone, leaving him to stare longingly after the receding fins.

Sorrells hadn't asked what that was all about and Helga hadn't offered an explanation. Not about the Fontaine woman or the telephone she'd had installed the week before. Mrs. Marston seemed to be changing by the day.

When Charlie left the mercantile, he was carrying T-shirts, two new pairs of Levis and assorted underwear and socks, but he was wearing his new boots. Helga's arms were also loaded down with purchases, which she placed on the floorboard of the pickup.

"Could you and Charlie find something to entertain yourselves for another half hour or so?" she asked. "Maybe run by the library and pick up the books Anita's saving for me? Oh, and tell her we're expecting her at the house Wednesday as soon as she can get there."

Helga was on the sidewalk and headed for Hannah's Hen Den when she added, "You're going to like those books, Charlie. At least I hope so. You would have read them if you'd been in school this year."

Sorrells and Charlie looked at each other. Sorrells appeared to be amused. Charlie's expression could best be described as tragic.

They returned to the pickup loaded down with books long before Helga came tripping out of Hannah Franklin's beauty parlor swishing her short blond hair and carrying two long golden braids. "I'm free!" she declared, "and I hope you like it, because I do." She pulled down the rearview mirror and smiled into it. "Oh dear," she said. "I could sure use a little makeup."

The two males in her immediate vicinity would need time to adjust. Hannah had warned Helga they might. "Men get used to what they see," she said, "and that's what they think they like. They come around after awhile."

"Looks nice," they both got around to mumbling, after which

— 48 —

Sorrells let Charlie drive them back to the ranch.

Helga sat in the middle and had to turn her knees towards Sorrells to allow Charlie to shift gears. Jake tried not to notice when her knees brushed against his, but she didn't much seem to care. In fact, she might have flashed him a playful grin. Sorrells couldn't be sure. He was staring straight ahead.

The old pickup was about a mile out of town when Charlie hit the brakes. The truck slid in the loose gravel, but he was able to keep it on the road. He had the door open before it rolled to a complete stop and was running back toward something only he had seen. Sorrells climbed out and held the door for Helga.

A dead dog lay beside the road, apparently hit by a car. Next to her lay a mixed breed puppy, whimpering as it nudged its mother. Charlie picked up the pup and cradled it in his arms while Sorrells looked around and found two more dead puppies, both victims of the car that had killed their mother.

Charlie walked back to the truck with the one surviving puppy, talking to it as he rubbed its fur.

"What're you doing, Charlie?" Sorrells question sounded like an accusation. If he had looked more closely, he would have seen that the boy was struggling to hold back tears.

"We can't leave him here. He'd die." There was defiance in Charlie's voice. Helga was proud of him.

"He's just a mutt. ..."

There was ice in Helga's voice when she said, "Mr. Sorrells, Charlie is right. We can't leave him here. We'll take him home with us. I'll try to get him to eat while you go back and bury the others."

Sorrells drove the rest of the way home while Helga and Charlie took turns holding the puppy. Women and kids, he was thinking as he headed to the barn for a shovel. What kind of person would kill a dog and her litter and leave the remains by the side of the road for someone else to take care of!

Charlie's thoughts took a different track. He was thinking those books Mrs. Marston ordered at the library might not be so bad after all. Maybe later he'd tell Mrs. Marston how much he really did like her hair.

Chapter Nine
Nightmares

The rain held off until late in the week, and then it came down in sheets. There would be little outdoor work that day, and maybe not for several days. Charlie and Pup lay curled up on Charlie's bunk, both of them sound asleep. It had been a hard night for all of them. Charlie had been up and down seeing to the dog's needs. Sorrells had been jarred awake in the night, haunted by memories, disoriented, craving the sting of liquor in his mouth and numbing the pain in his mind.

There was fire all around his position. Something had happened to his jump mates. He was lying in a wooded area, and the smell of stagnant water was in his nostrils. Nothing resembled the terrain the DZ maps had led him to expect. Flashes of light, tracers, screamed overhead and the anguished cries of injured and dying men assaulted his ears.

"Oh, God, where am I?" he cried out.

Charlie woke to find Sorrells sitting on the side of his cot, his T-shirt wet with sweat. He left Pup sleeping and crept toward his cot. "You okay, Mr. Sorrells?"

Jake tried to focus on the face before him, to understand what the phantom voice had said.

"Are you okay, Mr. Sorrells?" He turned his still unfocused eyes toward the sound. "That you, Charlie?"

"Yes sir. Are you sick or something?"

"Get me some water," he whispered.

He took the tin cup Charlie offered, then pushed past him and out the door. Lightning crackled on the horizon, followed by a distant rumble. Rain wasn't far off. He could smell it. The early October night air was cold on his feverish skin. He gulped the water, wishing to hell it was whiskey.

Jake knew the dreams meant trouble, and they'd been doubling up on him of late. He had lived with them so long that he knew they were warnings of things to come. First the overwhelming need for liquor, then the violence that followed. Only occasionally did the violence come first. It wasn't the memories he fought, it was the rage and the overwhelming desire for liquor that accompanied them.

Now he seldom slept well. Either he couldn't get to sleep or he woke in the middle of the night, got out of his bunk and walked, trying to force thoughts of the only thing that had ever helped from his mind.

He had been short with Charlie, and he was beginning to resent Mrs. Marston. Why had he come to this God forsaken place? He didn't owe her anything. If he knew where that worthless husband of hers was, he'd hunt him down, drag his ass back here and let the two of them fight it out on their own.

"Damn Eli Steigner for getting me into this mess," he shouted into the night. "Damn the Army Air Force, damn the V.A and the Germans who killed me!"

Helga heard Sorrells' pickup lumber past the house just after dawn the next morning, and turned the fire off under the skillet where breakfast bacon had begun to sizzle. She and Charlie would have oatmeal and toast later.

The roar of the pickup had no sooner faded into the distance than Charlie came into the kitchen carrying Pup, wrapped in a

THE GERMAN WOMAN'S HIRED HAND

blanket and whining for breakfast. Helga sat at the table with a cup of coffee. "Sit down, Charlie," she said. "We need to talk."

"Mr. Sorrells left in the pickup," he said, "and before that he was talking funny. Something about fire and guys screaming, and his T-shirt was sweaty. I brought him some water like he said, and then he went back to bed. He was gone when I got up, but I think he's sick."

Helga had been warned. She had seen this coming, had known it would be up to her to help Charlie understand. Somehow they must hold their lives together while they waited for Sorrells to work through the pain.

"I see," said Helga. "Yes, you could say Mr. Sorrells is sick. Sick in the worst way. Oh, Charlie, he fights it so hard, and most of the time he wins, but it could be that this time his addiction will beat him."

Her words hung between them while she poured warm milk into a bowl for Pup and handed Charlie a slice of bread to break up into it. He had come to grips with the meaning of her words before the toast browned and she set his oatmeal before him. Preoccupied with dark thoughts, Charlie set Pup on the floor in a corner beside the stove with his breakfast bowl.

Charlie had been happier here on the Marston Ranch than ever before in his life. But he had a working knowledge of what liquor could do, and none of it was good. His dad was sick like that, too, and he had gone off and left him on his own now and then. The last time, he hadn't come back.

"I'd best be getting the chores done," he said after awhile. "You think Pup'll be okay there in his box beside the stove?"

"Of course," Helga said, her hand on his shoulder. "And Charlie, please don't worry. It might not be all that bad this time. You're a good boy. Good for Mr. Sorrells and good for me, and Pup needs you too. You'll always have a place on the Marston Ranch, okay?"

Not trusting his voice, Charlie nodded and then headed for

the hen house, hurried on by a cacophony of clucking. Helga lifted the receiver, found the party line open, cranked up the operator, and placed two phone calls. One to Reverend Steigner, the other to Melba. Hopefully, Sorrells would drop by the cafe for breakfast. Maybe Melba would be able to keep him occupied until Eli could get there.

When the Steigners' phone rang, Eli threw back the covers and swung his feet to the floor. "I'll get it," he told his wife. "It's probably about old Mrs. Swanson's funeral. Don't get up."

Helga's voice was restrained, halting. "How soon can you get here?" she asked. "It looks like there's going to be trouble."

"Sorrells?" he asked.

"I'm afraid so," she said. "I don't like what Charlie told me about what happened out in the bunkhouse last night, and Jake tore out for town about an hour ago before breakfast. He's been acting strange lately. Surly. I have a bad feeling about this, Reverend Steigner. I'm afraid he's headed into what you warned me about."

"It sure sounds like it," he said. "You did the right thing to call me. Who's Charlie? Can he help you with Sorrells if he comes back to the ranch before I can get there?"

"Charlie is a fifteen year old boy who's helping out around here, but he's more than that. This is going to hit him hard. He thinks the world of Jake."

"I'll be there as soon as I can, but I have a funeral this morning, so it won't be before early afternoon. Can you handle things till then?"

"We'll do what we can. Charlie has gone through this often before with his father."

"Poor kid," he said. "Give me time to handle things here and I'll get there as soon as possible." Helga replaced the receiver and prepared herself for whatever might come.

Sorrells parked his pickup in front of the café and walked to

THE GERMAN WOMAN'S HIRED HAND

the storefront that housed the town's city hall, its one-man police department, and Deputy Roy Strange, the county deputy sheriff, a hometown boy. The deputy looked up as Sorrells stepped inside but offered no greeting as he moved toward the desk.

"My name is Jake Sorrells. I need some information."

"I know who you are. What kind'a information?"

"If you know who I am, then you know I work for Helga Marston."

"Yeah, I know that."

"Were you a deputy when John Marston went missing?"

"I was. I did some of the initial investigation."

"What can you tell me about John Marston's disappearance?"

Deputy Roy Strange leaned back in his chair and looked at Sorrells as if to determine whether or not his question was worth an answer.

"The German woman. She send you?"

"No. She doesn't know I'm here. What happened to her husband? She deserves that much. I'm going to get her an answer. What you need to decide now is whether you're going to help me or not."

Deputy Strange had heard the stories going around town. Enough to know this was not a man he wanted to have trouble with. Besides, Melba seemed to think he was okay.

"Sit down, Mr. Sorrells. We'll see what we can do." Deputy Strange went to a beat up file cabinet and pulled out a thin folder. He sat down at his desk and opened the Marston file. He was quiet for a minute, and then he started to read. "Marston is the son of a wealthy New England businessman. Marston returned from the war, apparently with no interest in the family business. There was a problem with a married woman. He was given his inheritance and purchased a ranch in Woodson County."

"So I've heard. What else?"

"His family isn't interested in pursuing the circumstances of his disappearance, and his wife doesn't have the funds even if she might be so inclined," said the deputy. "The sheriff made an attempt to investigate, but now he's lost interest. Most of us think Marston simply baled out on his wife."

An hour or more had gone by before they leaned back in their chairs, and by then they had developed a mutual respect for each other. Sorrells was convinced he could trust Deputy Strange to tell the facts on John Marston's disappearance as he saw them. It was clear that there was no indication that anyone in town bore Marston the kind of animosity that would lead to his murder. He had run up debts, but the Dibs locals would have no reason to remove their only hope of eventual collection.

Marston's car had not been found. If it were anywhere nearby, surely it would have been discovered by now.

"Anyone else go missing along about the same time?"

"You mean a female?"

"Yeah, I guess I do."

The deputy nodded. "That was the first thing we thought of. No, there wasn't anybody else. Not around here at least. That doesn't mean it didn't happen. But you know there ain't too many folks living around here, and everybody pretty much knows what everybody else is up to. If Marston left town because of a woman, she wouldn't be a local or live anywhere nearby."

"That sounds reasonable," Sorrells said. "Thanks for your help. One more thing, do your files have a description of Marston? Or better yet, a picture?"

"Yeah, but couldn't you get that kind'a stuff from his wife?"

"Probably, but I'm trying to handle this on my own."

The deputy slid a photo across the desk. Sorrells glanced at it and slipped it into his shirt pocket. "If Marston's alive," he said, "more than likely he's aligned himself with some sort of military connection."

"Makes sense."

"I've asked a friend to contact a couple of army legal service personnel he knew when he was an army chaplain. So far he's drawn a blank."

"Sounds like a long shot, but let me know what you come up with."

The two sat talking for a while longer, drinking putrid county coffee until Sorrells got up to leave.

"You a drink'n man, Mr. Sorrells? I got twenty-something quarts of moonshine I took off a couple of runners last night. Sure ain't gonna need that many for evidence. If you'd like a quart or two, you'd be welcome to 'em."

Shortly after noon, Melba placed a phone call to Helga. "Looks like you had it figured right when you phoned earlier," she said, and Helga knew what was coming.

"Is he there with you now?"

"He staggered in half an hour ago. Dad tried to keep him talking while I poured coffee down him, but he's too far gone for that. He's passed out in a booth, and I do mean out. I'm sorry, Helga. I'll get a couple of customers to load him into my car and bring him out to your place, if that's what you want."

"Thank you," said Helga. "Charlie's here and Reverend Steigner should be here soon. Right now I'm as concerned about Charlie as I am about Sorrells. That boy has already been through hell. He sure doesn't need this."

Chapter Ten
Relapse

E li pulled up to the ranch house in the early afternoon. He knocked once, then opened the door and went inside. A teenage boy sat at the kitchen table, a puppy in his lap.

"You must be Charlie," he said.

"Yes sir. Are you the preacher who's Mr. Sorrells' friend?"

"I am. Where is Mrs. Marston?"

"She's in there with Mr. Sorrells." Charlie pointed to Helga's closed bedroom door.

Steigner opened the door to find her sitting in a straight-back chair, her head resting against a small cushion. "Helga?" he whispered. "It's Eli."

She rolled her head toward him and opened her eyes. "I'm glad you're here," she said. "Did you meet Charlie? I don't know what I'd have done without him."

Sorrells lay on his side, his eyes closed, his breathing even. Helga moved toward Steigner where he stood looking down on his troubled friend.

"God help him," he said. "How long has he been like this?"

"If you mean how long has he been … drunk, since about noon, I think. He's been asleep for about an hour."

"How did you get him home?"

"Strangest thing. One of Ed Mason's boys drove him here in Melba's car, and the other one followed in Sorrells' pickup. It was all they could do to get him into the house. I supposed those two would be the last to help us after what happened at their dad's feed store."

"How long did they stay?"

"Long enough to see that Charlie and I could handle it. At first he was uncooperative, but we eventually got him cleaned up and into bed. He moans and thrashes about, then speaks incoherently, but mostly he's been like this. Still as death. He had been in town only a short time before Melba found him slumped in a booth."

"That's good. In extreme cases, he might be drunk for a week. He should be a lot easier to handle this time. Do you know what might have set him off?"

"Charlie told me at breakfast that Jake has been having nightmares. I know he has been acting different, upset with Charlie and me over little things, but nothing that should have caused this."

"He's an alcoholic, Helga. That's all it takes."

They closed the bedroom door behind them and joined Charlie in the kitchen.

"I have coffee," she said.

"That would be wonderful," he replied.

As she carried two ironstone cups to the table, he added, "I hope you are well supplied with coffee. Chances are you'll need a lot of it."

Helga glanced at Eli above the rim of her cup. "You've mentioned his war experiences. Don't you think you should tell me more?" Charlie moved as if to excuse himself, but she raised her hand to detain him. "Perhaps you need to hear this as well," she said, and Charlie sat down.

"I think you're right," Eli said. "His care is in your hands now, and you both have a right to know."

"Jake Sorrells was a member of the 101st Airborne Division, the Screaming Eagles. You may have noticed a tattoo on his shoulder."

Helga nodded. "A parachutist," said Charlie, his interest whetted. "He told me that's what they're called."

"Sorrells was one of thousands of men who were parachuted behind German lines as part of the Allied Invasion of Normandy. Their mission, simply stated, was to disrupt German attempts to reinforce their lines at Normandy, and to capture Cherbourg in order to provide the Allies a port of supply. To do that, men like Sorrells were to be dropped at night into the middle of hostile forces. I will tell you that a lot of things can go wrong in the heat of battle, and this battle was the largest in history. Although the men were well trained, a nighttime drop of this size was untested. It has been a long time since, and it's never been tried again.

"The Army had sent out smaller groups called Pathfinders the night before. They were to plant beacons that would mark the proper drop zones for the C-47 aircraft to drop their troops the following night. Most of these beacons failed for one reason or the other. The consequence was that most of the airborne troops, including Jake Sorrells, were dropped in the wrong place and in the face of overwhelming enemy fire. Sorrells told me that as far as he knows, he was the only man in his plane to reach the ground alive.

"Sorrells had been dropped somewhere east of the Merderet River in a swamp. He hid for hours in the dark as German troops looked for any Airborne soldiers that had survived. He knew that he must leave his position while it was still dark, so he crawled through the wet grass for miles till he ran into other Airborne personnel dropped from other planes and surrounded by the enemy. He couldn't fire his rifle because the sound would reveal his position, but he told me he killed several enemy soldiers that first night with his bare hands or with his knife."

"He sure knows how to fight!" Charlie interjected.

"That's come up in several of our conversations before," Eli replied. "He had the same training as all the others, he just paid more attention."

"Do you think that's what it is?" Charlie asked.

"Perhaps some of it." Reverend Steigner paused before adding, "But I'm afraid he has an unnatural talent for violence. There's a lot more to the story, but it would do you no service to hear it. Suffice it to say that Jake Sorrells experienced more hell in those few days than most men face in a lifetime. He was near death when he was found, but his scars tell the story better than I can."

"Reverend Steigner, how did he get those wounds?" Helga asked.

"He literally blew himself up," Steigner said bluntly. "Held the enemy off long enough to do the job he had come to do, but too long for him to get away."

The clock ticked loudly in the otherwise silent room, then chimed four times before anyone spoke.

"We should probably let him sleep," said Eli, "but I think I need to be the one who gets him up. That may not be something you need to be involved with. Why don't you make another pot of coffee? I'll go see what I can do."

Eli returned to the bedroom, leaving the door ajar. When Helga glanced in, she saw the Reverend on his knees beside the bed in prayer. Later, there was a shuffling at the bedroom door and Eli emerged supporting his friend, moving cautiously toward the kitchen. The whites of Sorrells eyes were blood red, unseeing.

Helga got up from the table where she had been helping Charlie with his reading. *Treasure Island* might be the breakthrough she had hoped it would be. At least he was interested enough to ask the meanings of words he didn't know.

Eli situated Sorrells at the table where their coffee waited, and where Charlie read aloud while Helga sewed buttons on one of the dozens of patchwork jackets she was preparing to send to Clarissa Fontaine. Orders kept coming in. Too many for only two seamstresses to handle, and Melba wasn't much help. She agreed to cut out the irregular pieces of cloth and handle the bookwork, but a needle in

Melba's hand was dangerous.

    Helga sighed. And now this. Was she up to it? Could she be what Jake Sorrells and the boy needed for her to be? Pup whined in his corner. She motioned for Charlie to keep on reading and got up to fill his dish.

Chapter Eleven
Things Change

After Sorrells lost the bout with his demons, things might have gone on much as usual at the Marston ranch had he been inclined to return to the bunk house. But he was not so inclined, and life took a strange twist. Nothing would be the same for any of them by the month's end.

Charlie was nowhere to be found when Eli left the ranch at dusk that first day. He had taken Pup and his book out to the bunkhouse soon after the Reverend concluded Sorrells' story. He had some thinking to do. Pup romped throughout the one big room, glad to be back in familiar territory. The bunkhouse was home to both of them, and Sorrells and Helga were the closest thing to family Charlie had ever known.

He looked about at six bunks neatly made up, floors he scrubbed daily, four unadorned windows with glass so clear he could see as far as the rise of ground, and he envisioned the pond beyond. But why envision when the air was clear and a fantastic Oklahoma sunset was building? He dropped the book on his bunk and went out into the evening with Pup at his heels.

Prairie dogs poked their heads up out of their holes at intervals all throughout the pastureland, then scurried back under with Pup yipping at their retreat. A hawk swooped down and scooped up a mouse, three jackrabbits stood like statues in a group. A slithering in the grass sent Pup into retreat and set Charlie to watching where he stepped, and then there it was: the spring-fed pond, gorged by the early rain that had filled the reservoir up north and sent the water rushing down.

Charlie sat leaning against the tree trunk Sorrells had leaned against the day he mapped the Marston ranch and found it in need of care. Pup begged to play fetch and Charlie obliged, throwing the same twig over and over again. Things changed. Charlie would be sixteen in the spring, and he had learned some things along the way.

He could only vaguely remember the face of the woman who had been his mother, but he remembered all too clearly the harsh hands of his father. Charlie had lived an undisciplined life, in school for short periods of time and then not. At first he had counted himself lucky to be free of constraints, but that was before he experienced the pleasure in a job well done. He had admired Jake Sorrells and wanted to please him. Wanted to be him, a man short on words but long on action. A man who could stand up for himself in a remarkable way, who could mend a fence, brand a calf, jerry-rig a pickup into working order and then teach him to drive it.

Sorrells trusted him to complete man-sized jobs and helped him do them over again when he failed, but he was also a man who woke screaming in the night and rose drenched in sweat. Sorrells had failed them all when he yielded to his demons. Now he was not himself, but he was struggling to regain control.

That was going to be a man-sized job. Sorrells had done it wrong, and the least Charlie could do was help him do it over again. It was no more than Sorrells would do for him. He whistled Pup to his side and turned his back on the last of the sunset. "Let's go home," he said. "It's going to be all right."

Earlier that evening, Charlie had no sooner picked up his book and left with Pup for the bunkhouse than Sorrells staggered into the kitchen to sit at the table, his head in his hands.

"Where's Eli?" he asked, his voice muffled against his chest.

"He had to get back for a meeting," said Helga, making her voice light. "Is there something I can get for you? An aspirin? More coffee? Here, you're soaking wet. Let me help you off with that shirt. There. I'll just run out to the bunkhouse and get you a clean one."

When he didn't answer, she turned the fire down under the stew simmering on the back of the stove and made the short trip to the bunkhouse and back with several changes of clothing. He sat where she had left him, but his eyes met hers head on. That's better, she thought. Still bloodshot, but lightening up a bit. Maybe he was over the worst of it.

She smiled in a way she hoped was encouraging. "Stew's almost ready," she said. "Charlie wasn't in the bunkhouse. That boy does enjoy tromping through the pasture with that dog. I'll take his dinner out to him later. Maybe he'll read while he's eating." Her laugh bordered on hysteria, but she went on. "He's making great headway, and Melba thinks he has a head for numbers. I just hope it'll be enough to get him enrolled with the others next year. It won't be easy to keep him in school if they put him in with the younger kids. I guess we'll just have to wait and. ..."

She might have rambled on into the night, filling the uncomfortable void with her voice, if Sorrells hadn't gently grasped her wrist and turned her toward him. "It's okay, Helga," he said softly. "I'm not Marston. I won't hurt you. I just need to stay here in the house, away from Charlie for a while. He's lived with drunks his whole life. Now he's found a home with people he thought he could trust. Give me a little time to get over this, and I'll be on my way."

Helga had never before heard him string so many words together. His need must be even greater than she feared. She knelt by the side of his chair and said, "I was afraid that's what you were thinking. Oh, Jake, don't you know how important you've been to us? How important you still are and always will be to Charlie and me? He forgives you for stumbling, and I've found nothing in you I need to forgive. He and I will both do what we can to help you. We're a bit like family, don't you think? Not even the best of those are perfect."

She pulled out the chair beside him and clasped his hand in both of hers. He didn't draw away. "Let's get this straight right now," she said, her voice firm. "I don't know what love is and I don't suppose you do either. What I feel for you is complicated, but I do have feelings. I don't know where that might go and I don't care. It's enough that you're here now.

"You've shown me a life I sometimes think I'd like to live on a permanent basis, but you're like quicksilver, Jake. You could be gone tomorrow, and I'd never try to stop you. Don't think about leaving right away. When you're up to it, there will be cattle to work and the ranch to run, but there's no hurry. Charlie and I can handle it till you're ready to.

"Now let's get that shirt changed and we'll have our supper. Maybe later I'll rub your back until you can get to sleep. And no more dreams, Jake. I'll be there beside you. I'll know when they're coming, and I'll wake you before they take hold. I'll be there afterwards to comfort you until the memories fade, and if Eli's God is good, one day those dreams will die."

Even if Sorrells had been a man of words, Helga's intensity would have rendered him speechless. He looked into the lovely face that opened up to him and regretted all the lost days of his life. If only. ... But, no, dead men didn't get second chances. She had no idea of the life he had lived these past years, how much havoc he had created in the line of his work, or how much he had enjoyed that work.

Unwilling or unable to route the demons from his own life, Sorrells had devoted his efforts toward cleaning up other people's messes. The job paid well, but he knew what a dangerous man he had become and how dangerous were those he encountered along the way. People like Sorrells had enemies. He wondered how much Helga had guessed. Not much, he supposed. A woman like her, one who had already suffered so much, would never put up with a man like him, and he wasn't looking to give up any of it. Still, the promise of a back rub and a pretty woman to curl up with did seem a whole lot like a second chance.

Sorrells picked up a clean shirt and was headed for the windmill trough on shaky legs when Helga stopped him. "You're too unsteady on your feet for that," she said. "Can't have my hired hand drowning in the cattle's drinking trough. I'll take Charlie's supper out to him, and I'll run a tub of hot water for you when I get back. A little civilization never hurts, and I promise it's the last favor I'll ask of you."

Helga carried a heavily laden tray to the bunkhouse, and Pup barked a welcome even before she stepped through the door. Charlie looked up from his book and grinned. "How's Mr. Sorrells doing now?" he asked. "Is he feeling better, do you think?"

"I believe he is somewhat better, Charlie. He hasn't eaten yet, but he says he's hungry. Can you and Pup hold things down out here if Mr. Sorrells stays at the house for a few days?"

Charlie nodded with forced solemnity. "You bet," he said. "Pup is good company, and we're all fixed up out here. Got everything we need. See you in the morning," he added, returning to his book. When the bunkhouse door closed behind her, Charlie grinned broadly.

Sorrells' appetite returned with a vengeance. He enjoyed every bite right down to the soda biscuits that soaked up the last of the broth, and then he polished it all off with a chunk of Helga's berry pie. She put their dishes in the sink to soak, then sat down beside him. "Finish your coffee," she said. "I'll start your bathwater. Just remember," she finished with a twinkle, "we're not traveling a one way street here. You can start my bath the next time."

Sorrells examined the dregs at the bottom of his cup as the sound of running water filled the house and the hot water heater popped in the closet behind him. What in hell was he doing, and who was that woman? The whole damn town must have noticed her change over the past few months. Who the hell wouldn't? He sure had, but what was this all about? Not that he objected. If he'd figured it right, what fool would?

"Ready?" she said from behind him, and he tried to tell himself he hadn't started at the sound of her voice. Not him. Not the ever-vigilant Sorrells, always alert to danger from any and all directions. Well, he had and she knew it. He could see it in her smile as she placed her hands on his shoulders, and that was another thing. Where had that smile been hiding inside this complicated woman?

Wild horses couldn't keep him from finding out. He took her hands from his shoulders, but relinquished only one. "You lead the way," he thought he said, though he hardly recognized his own voice.

The bathroom was steamy, inviting. He stepped into the claw-footed enamel tub and, little by little, settled into hot water until it rose to his shoulders. He closed his eyes, leaned back against the curve of the tub and, enjoying the sensation of abandon, turned this first step of the evening's program over to Helga. How long had it been since he had allowed himself this sort of pleasure? The lapping of almost-hot water against his skin, the odor of perfumed soap in his nostrils, the rough cloth gliding over his body beneath a gentle force? Maybe he never had.

Helga continued her ministrations until the water began to cool, and then she dried him thoroughly with thick, warm towels. When she was satisfied that not a damp spot remained, she guided him to the bed. It had never given her the pleasure that she anticipated she was about to experience with this man who thought he was dead but, considering the changes that were transpiring beneath her touch, she was certain was not.

Sorrells suffered no dreams that night and, for the same reason, not the next night or the next, but neither of them was fooled. The dreams would be back, possibly worse than ever, but Helga was gathering ammunition. She would be ready. Sorrells' hauntings, if they came, would never have encountered so formidable a force as Helga Heinke Marston in defense of what she valued.

And then one morning Sorrells buckled his jeans, pulled on his boots and headed out early to wake Charlie and Pup. In Sorrells' absence, Charlie had shown himself to be a good hand, and also discreet. Not by word or glance did he indicate his awareness of the change that had transpired on the Marston ranch. The cattle had been fed and watered on schedule, and Charlie had even secured a couple of loose fences. Between times, he had kept to his books. Helga and Melba would be as proud of the progress he had made in his bookwork as Sorrells was of the care he had taken of the ranch.

Chapter Twelve
Community Acceptance

News travels fast in a town the size of Dibs, and acceptance comes in curious ways. Wherever the locals gathered, Jake Sorrells' was being analyzed, his actions debated and judged. He wasn't all that unlike them after all. The man who passed out in Clem's Cafe booth could be forgiven by all but the staunchest teetotaler, and more than one of them had been drunk out of his mind a time or two.

Ranchers noted that he was turning the Marston place around, and business owners saw his success as a paying proposition. One that promised to produce enough cash to pay off the debts John Marston had left them holding. Sure, he was hotheaded and fast with his hands, but he hadn't done Les Jones anymore harm than any one of them would have done on occasion if he'd been man enough. Besides, that kid, Charlie Conn, sure hadn't deserved the treatment Jones handed out.

Sorrells' most unexpected defense came from Ed Mason and his sons, all three of whom he had laid out on the feed store floor. That episode had apparently served as a wake up call. Mason no longer spent his days playing dominoes with his friends in the pool hall. He sometimes dropped by, but after the incident at his store, he had made the decision to cut back on his daily consumption of beer. He

THE GERMAN WOMAN'S HIRED HAND

and his boys grew to consider the matter an embarrassment and wanted it behind them.

At first, the two Mason boys, Sid and Fred, had threatened to become part of the local folklore, but not in a good way. They were the ones who had actually fought the mysterious Jake Sorrells. Over the next several weeks, as their bruises healed, they recounted the story many times over to willing listeners until it began to ring hollow even in their own ears and, to their credit, honesty won out.

"There ain't no doubt but what we got our asses whipped," they had begun to joke among those who gathered at the feed store to discuss the high school football team's latest achievement. As time went on, being laid low by the mysterious Jake Sorrells became a badge of honor, and they were the first to laugh at themselves.

For Helga and Charlie, those first days after Sorrells moved into the house passed not unlike the days before. She put meals on the table and kept up with the laundry, and Charlie kept up with all that the ranch required. Neither of them dared think ahead to a time when the ranch would require more than an almost-sixteen-year-old boy could handle with an occasional assist from Helga, but she wasn't counting Sorrells out. On the morning a week after his drinking bout, he had proven himself worthy of her confidence when he resumed work on the Marston ranch.

Helga was finishing up the breakfast dishes when the phone rang, two shorts and a long. It was Elsie Mason, Ed's wife, and she got right down to business.

"About Mr. Sorrells," she said, "My Ed was like that and getting worse. Then, thanks to what happened at the store that morning, he saw that the boys were going down that road, too, and he gave up on his own. Liquor, I mean. Even joined the church. I'm beholden to Mr. Sorrells for what he done that day for all three of 'em, though it could'a been me threatening to leave. I'd packed my bag and bought me a one-way bus ticket to the City where my sister lives before he come around. I suspect it's his respect for my cooking that done it, but Ed's claiming it's what went on down at the store that day. Anyhow, it was him that sent the boys to bring Mr. Sorrells out to the ranch when Melba called, and I got a refund on that bus ticket the same day."

Helga might have tried to get a word in edgewise if she hadn't been speechless. "You've got your hands full with him right now," Elsie went on. "I've been there and I know. So do most'a the women in the guild, so we're going to see that you don't need to cook for a while. It's the least we can do. Is there anything else you need?"

When Helga could trust her voice, she said, "Mrs. Mason, it's kind of you to offer to bring in food, but things are pretty much back to normal here now. There is something I've been meaning to talk to you about, though, and this might be as good a time as any. Melba and I have a project underway, and we could use your help and a little help from your boys, too. I'd appreciate it if they could come pick up a dozen big boxes that need to get mailed to California before the end of the week. You remember Melba's friend, Sadie Dale? Well, she calls herself Clarissa Fontaine now, and she's big into the West Coast fashion world.

"If things work out like we plan, there'll be work for any Dibs woman who can sew and is willing to gamble her time on this venture of ours. It won't cost them a cent, and it's looking like it might work into something profitable for all of us. I've got three dozen patchwork jackets, that many purses and twice that many sofa pillows ready for the market, and orders for twice that many more."

Elsie was a good listener, and she didn't miss a beat. "If it's anything like the crazy quilts most of our grandmothers taught us to make when we was kids," she said, "sure, I could give it a try. I'll pass the word on to the ladies of the guild, and we'll talk more when I bring out my tuna casserole. Might as well. It's on the counter cooling.

"There's pie that Hannah at the beauty shop made, too. She's proud of what she did to your hair back a'ways, and she expressly asked that I bring her back a report. Might not'a baked that pie if I'd refused, so I'll see you along about noon.

"Oh, and Helga, the boys are on their way now to pick up those packages you need to have mailed. They will be, anyway, once I tell them. Sounds like they'll have a truck bed full of 'em."

Chapter Thirteen
Thanksgiving

A ray of light filtered through the clear glass insert in the stained glass window to lie upon the bowed head of Helga Marston. Thanksgiving was only a few days away, and at Mary Steigner's invitation, she had left Jake and Charlie to sleep in and had come to attend Sunday services at the Woodson Lutheran Church. Helga had silently concluded her personal prayer of gratitude when the organ swelled into "Blessed Be the Tie That Binds," and she and Mary had been swept into the vestibule where the Reverend Eli Steigner stood greeting the departing congregation.

"Oh, Mr. Sinclair," Mary called out to a tall, dapper if somewhat effeminate middle-aged man, "I want you to meet my dear friend, Helga Marston. Helga, this is Woodson's new postmaster, Howard Sinclair. He's been here only a month and doesn't know many of us yet, but we're so pleased to have him."

"An honor to meet you," he said bowing over the hand she offered, "an honor indeed." Well-built woman, he was thinking; this side of thirty; no wedding band; wonder how she supports herself.

Helga withdrew her hand and turned to Mary. "Thanks for inviting me to the services," she said, "and tell Eli I enjoyed his stirring message. I've got to run now. Sunday or not, after lunch there'll be jackets and sofa pillows to box up for tomorrow's shipment, and I'm behind on my bookwork."

"An intriguing accent," simpered the postmaster. "French, isn't it?"

"German," said Helga and turned to Mary. "Don't forget now, she said, "I'll see you and Eli out at the ranch Thursday at 12 o'clock sharp. That's early for a Thanksgiving dinner, but it wouldn't do for the Reverend to be late for the Church's traditional Thanksgiving festivities that evening."

"No indeed," beamed Mary, and at that point her Christian charity overpowered her usual good manners. "Oh, Mr. Sinclair," she said, "what a shame it would be if you were left to spend Thanksgiving Day alone! Why not ride out to the Marston Ranch for dinner with us?"

Hmm, thought the conniving Howard Sinclair. Dine at the table of the lovely Mrs. Marston, who owns a ranch and doubtless hundreds of heads of cattle plus a business on the side?

"Delighted," he said with another of his quaint bows. "It will be my pleasure to not only attend but to provide the afternoon's entertainment — an extensive slide show compiled from photos taken throughout my travels." He stepped back a pace and doffed his hat, finishing with, "Until then, ladies, I'll leave you."

"Oh dear," said Mary from behind the hand she had, too late, clamped to her mouth. "What have I done?"

Helga patted her shoulder but was laughing too hard to reply, and she laughed even harder as she climbed into Sorrell's pickup in the parking lot. *Delighted* indeed, she thought. Would Mr. Howard Sinclair, postmaster extraordinaire, be so delighted to snap up Mary's ill-fated invitation if he could see her behind the wheel of this monster belching smoke as she pulled it onto the highway? Helga might be a foreigner, but she'd seen the glint in the postmaster's eye, and she was no fool.

Helga had determined that Thanksgiving dinner at the Marston

Ranch, Charlie's first ever, would be a culinary delight this year. Also somewhat of a miracle, considering the demands her budding fashion enterprise were making on her time. Pup had been ecstatic over all the new smells for a solid week prior to the festivities, and it had seemed to Charlie to be snowing flour in the kitchen throughout those days and sometimes into the night. He was no less excited than Pup. They could both see that Helga intended the day to be memorable.

She would put the leaf in the kitchen table and cover it with the linen cloth. The kitchen would be cozier than the dining room, which there had never been an occasion to use. Besides, she didn't have the proper tableware it required, but she would by Christmas. For now, she would make up for the lack of ambiance by loading the kitchen table with the fruits of her labor and be thankful for the life she had never dared to dream of.

Finally the big day arrived. A joyful Pup was allowed back into the kitchen where the succulent odors had taken shape, and where he might reach them if he could leap high enough. Helga couldn't read Jake's face, but Charlie's was wide eyed and expectant when the Reverend and his wife arrived, their guest in the front seat because, as Mary later said, he insisted he got car sick if he rode in the back.

Mary waved enthusiastically through the back window, but Eli seemed somewhat less cheerful. Howard Sinclair — who had alighted first and gained the front porch where Charlie waited to greet the guests — had apparently not made a pleasant passenger. "Here, boy," the postmaster barked, "bring in the boxes you'll find on the back seat and be careful. They contain a valuable slideshow and projector."

If any of the others had heard the tone of Howard's voice, the day's festivities would have ended there. Howard's Civil Service rating had earned him a postmaster position on the Oklahoma plains, but he was not thrilled with the appointment, or with anything else.

When Jake saw the Steigners' car pull up he came in from the

THE GERMAN WOMAN'S HIRED HAND

barn to greet his friend Eli and was disturbed by the unaccustomed frown on his face. Eli might have explained the cause, but Helga was at the door calling them all in to dinner. And what a dinner it was, complete with succulent turkey stuffed with sage dressing and all the trimmings any worthy Thanksgiving dinner calls for, but infinitely better.

Howard surveyed the heavily laden table without comment, but frowned when the hired hands took their seats at the table and suggested that Pup be banished to the yard.

He took the seat Helga gestured toward and waited until Eli had asked the blessing before carefully polishing his cutlery with the immaculate white napkin beside his plate. Jake looked from the postmaster to the strangely subdued Charlie sitting across the table from him and knew Mary's guest was on his way to ruining the boy's first ever Thanksgiving dinner.

If table conversation lagged, it wasn't for lack of Howard's running account of the persecutions he suffered daily in his line of work: For one thing, old Mrs. Parsley misdirecting the mail delivered to her boarding house residents, and if that wasn't enough, those stupid letters to Santa clogging the post office in-box, to say nothing of the town of Woodson itself: an absolute dearth of entertainment, and he ventured to guess even less in Dibs, and how could a classy lady like Helga bear being stuck out here in no-man's land with no social life whatsoever.

At that point, Jake laid down his fork, caught Charlie's eye and said, "Time for us hired hands to get back to work. Thank you kindly, Mrs. Marston, for a very fine meal."

Helga nodded and held her tongue out of respect for a mortified Mary, whose guest Howard was, and poor Eli all but wept that he couldn't join Jake and Charlie in the bunkhouse where he figured rightly they were going to listen to the football game on the Philco radio he knew was out there.

When Howard asked for a white sheet to pin up on the living room wall so he could get his slideshow underway, Mary clutched her head and laid claim to a migraine; Eli grabbed up the boxes Charlie had brought inside, offered Helga a sheepish grin, and headed for the car. "Come along, Mr. Sinclair," he called back over his shoulder, "the little pilgrims will be aligning themselves against the Indians if I'm not at the church in less than an hour."

Helga cleaned up the kitchen, loaded trays with leftovers and two pies that hadn't been touched, threw a coat over her shoulders and made her way to the bunkhouse, where laughter and barking and the sound of Detroit trouncing the Packers 52-35 in a Thanksgiving Day football game that history would record as one of the finest, held sway.

Charlie's first Thanksgiving hadn't been what Helga wanted for him, but the three of them had more or less spent it together, and God willing, there would be others.

Chapter Fourteen
Trouble at Boys Ranch

The December weather was growing colder with each day that passed, but Sorrells had been told that in this part of Oklahoma snow and cold weather would arrive in January and February. Each day he and Charlie had loaded the flat bed truck with hay and cattle feed to help the stock survive on the limited amount of available grass. Much of Helga's time was now spent in town in response to her rapidly expanding business. Sorrells had anticipated much the same thing would be true for the next few months. Then one day an unexpected visit from Eli Steigner had changed everything.

Sorrells was in the barn loft throwing hay down to the bed of the truck. Often as not they bounced off and Charlie picked them up and returned them to the bed.

Sorrells saw Eli's car pull in by the side of the bunkhouse and he climbed down from the loft to greet his only real friend. The wind was blowing and cold so he suggested that Eli come into the bunk house for a cup of coffee.

"Helga's in town," he said. "She spends a lot of her time there these days."

"So I've heard," Eli replied. "Who would have ever guessed all this could have happened?"

Sorrells changed the subject. "Have you heard anything new

about Marston?"

"No, but I'm close. I came here because of a letter I received. It's from a man who says he's an old friend of yours. I knew that would be rare, so I thought you would be interested." Eli handed the envelope to Sorrells.

The letter was addressed to Eli Steigner and its return address was Baptist Boys Ranch, Century, Wyoming. Underneath the printed words was the handwritten signature of Buck Thomas. "He is an old friend," Sorrells commented as he unfolded the letter. It was written on lined legal-size yellow paper and in pencil. It read:

"Dear Reverend Steigner, it's been several years, but the last time I heard from Jake Sorrells he told me he made his living solving problems the people that hired him could not do for themselves. I got one of those problems here at the Ranch. He told me if I ever needed anything to let you know and you could probably get in touch with him. Tell Jake there's people up here trying to convince the Baptists to sell them the Ranch, and that the preacher who's the current administrator is way over his head trying to convince them to let us be. I'm not real sure what Jake meant by solving problems, but know'n Jake, I figger he'd never say anything he couldn't back up.

"If you have any luck in getting in touch with him, please ask him to get here just as soon as he can. Tell him I ain't gonna let these kids here, who ain't done nothing wrong, be taken over by the state and shipped off to some state institution." The letter ended, "Much obliged, Buck Thomas."

"I wonder what that means?" Eli asked.

"I don't know." Sorrells set the letter aside. "But Buck Thomas was as close to a father as I'll ever have."

"What are you going to do?" Eli asked.

"I'm not sure. Probably go to Century, Wyoming. I'll see if I can reach Buck on the phone. Let's go up to the house."

Jake asked the long distance operator to connect him with

Wyoming information. The Wyoming operator looked up the Baptist Boys Ranch number and agreed to forward the call. When the line was answered, she told the person on the line that there was a person-to-person call for Mr. Buck Thomas, and a few minutes later Buck was on the line.

"Buck," Sorrells said, "this is Jake. I hear you got a problem."

"Jake, thank God. You know I wouldn't bother you if there was anybody else that could help us. When can you get here?"

"What kind of problem other than some people want to buy the ranch?" Sorrells asked.

"Jake, I done spent two weeks in the hospital for speak'n up to what they're trying to do. They damn near beat me to death."

There was a pause before Jake responded. "Buck, don't do anything till I get there. I'll be leaving as soon as I can. Listen to me. Don't do anything. I'll call you where to meet me."

"Bless you, Jake," Buck Thomas said as the line went dead.

"What can I do to help?" Eli asked.

"My old truck can't make it anywhere near that far," Jake answered. "Besides, Helga and Charlie need it more than me. You can take me back to Woodson. I'll try to catch a bus to where I can get a train going north."

"Maybe I could take you to Wyoming," Eli offered.

Sorrells looked at his only friend as if he had made a bad joke. He was almost laughing when he replied. "Eli, I appreciate the offer, but what the hell are you thinking? You know very well the last thing I'd need is a preacher with me."

"You've no doubt made a good point." Eli couldn't manage a return of Jake's grin. "What will I tell Helga?"

"Not a damn thing. Charlie either, except that I know I'm not through here and I'll be back as soon as I can. They need to understand that some day I won't be back, but that time hasn't come."

Eli followed Sorrells back to the bunkhouse to pack a few things in his duffel bag and to take a fist full of cash from under his mattress and cram it into the pocket of a clean pair of jeans that he was putting on. "Give me a minute," he told Eli. Sorrells crossed to the barn, to his storage place, and opened its lock. From his arsenal he removed a .45 Army Colt and put it in the band of his jeans. Then he looked for Charlie.

"Charlie, I'm going to have to leave for awhile. I expect you to take care of things till I get back."

Charlie's eyes widened. "You're coming back, aren't you, Jake?"

Sorrells was not a man to demonstrate affection, but this time he made an exception. His hand clamped over Charlie's shoulder, "Just as soon as I can," he said.

During the drive to Woodson, Eli raised the subject of the relationship between Helga and Jake. "You know that girl loves you, don't you?"

It took Sorrells a minute to respond. "Maybe she thinks she does, but I'm carrying way too much baggage for any woman to have to bear. Nobody knows that more than you do, Eli. We both know she would be better off without me. Charlie too, for that matter."

It was with considerable trepidation that Eli left Jake Sorrells at the Woodson bus station. Then he went by the parsonage to get Mary to accompany him back to the ranch in order for someone to be there when Helga returned from Dibs.

True to his word, Eli was back at the ranch when Helga drove into the yard, the pickup bed loaded with purchases and a welcoming smile on her face. Eli relayed Jake's message regarding the Wyoming letter that required Jake's immediate attention, and then hurried back to Woodson where an emergency board meeting was already underway at the church. Something to do with the town's postmaster, the board president had said.

Charlie was a study in dejection as he came from the barn to see if Helga needed him to unload the pickup, shoulders slumped, dragging steps, not a glimmer of light in his eyes. "Reverend Eli took Jake to the bus station so we could use the pickup while he's gone," said Charlie, his chin all but resting on his chest. "He's gon'na try to get back by Christmas, he says, but..."

Helga had been distressed by Eli's message too, but suddenly her maternal instincts took hold. She grabbed Charlie by the shoulders and said, "Listen to me, Charlie Conn, we didn't let that idiot Howard Sinclair ruin our Thanksgiving and we're damn sure not going to let Jake Sorrells ruin our Christmas. You get the stuff in the back of this pickup unloaded and be careful, some of it's breakable. Then find a saw and a sharp ax in the barn and throw them into the truck bed. You and I are going to cut us a Christmas tree and haul it to the house, and then I'm going to teach you how to make peanut brittle and divinity. We'll listen to Christmas music while we decorate the tree, so bring in the Philco from the bunkhouse while I change into my work clothes. Christmas is going to happen in less than two weeks, and we're going to be ready for it. Now scat!"

Charlie had been as much shocked by Helga's "damn" as he'd been overwhelmed by the flurry of instructions that followed, but he managed to do all Helga had asked. He and Pup were in the pickup waiting for whatever came next when she flew out of the house and wrenched open the pickup door. "Watch out, trees, here we come," she called out gaily, and Charlie noticed she had attached a red bow to the top of her wooly cap. With a twinkle in her eye, she pulled down the earflaps and grinned with Charlie over the ridiculous spectacle she was making of herself, and Pup joined the foolishness at the top of his lungs. Helga's attitude was contagious. Charlie had been somber, mulling over all he had learned in the past half hour about the versatility of women, but now he revved up the engine, determined to join in the fun.

By bus and by train, it took Sorrells almost two miserable days and one night to reach Casper, Wyoming. He made his way to a nearby hotel and registered under an assumed name. He asked the man at the desk for a dollar's worth of nickels and went to the lobby pay phone to call Buck Thomas, asking him if it might be possible to pick him up.

"I can come right now!" Buck offered.

"No, don't do that. I need some sleep. Tomorrow will be fine." He added, "Buck, don't tell a soul I'm coming. Never mention my name. In fact, let me give you the name I'm listed under here at the hotel."

The next day Sorrells had slept till noon when the phone rang to tell him he had a visitor who asked to see him. Sorrells told the clerk to send him up. Sorrells had just stepped out of the shower when there was a knock at the door. "It's open," he yelled out, "come on in." He was standing at the bathroom door, a damp towel wrapped around his hips, when Buck Thomas opened the door and stepped inside. Sorrells had not seen him in several years.

At seventy-five years of age, except for the bruises and lacerations he had recently sustained, Buck had somehow managed to stay pretty much the same as he had been when Sorrells was a kid: still slender, maybe a bit bent over, his mustache was white, a few deep wrinkles due to hours spent in the winter winds or hot summers, but all in all he was still the same as Sorrells remembered.

Sorrells had changed from kid to a man, but that was not what Buck first noticed. "My God, boy!" he exclaimed, "what happened to your chest?"

"I guess you could say I sorta blew myself up, Buck, but you are looking good, considering you just got out of the hospital. What happened to you?"

Buck was still staring at Sorrells' chest. "I heard you was some kind of hero. Where you get them damn scars?"

"I got those at Normandy, Buck. Sit down and tell me exactly what's happened while I get dressed."

"There's this guy came up here from Denver a few years back when the oil play and coal mining cranked up after the war. He calls hisself Edward Phelps. Says he's a lease speculator. Anyways, he's bought up any minerals he can, oil and coal or both. He came to the Boys Ranch and said he wanted to lease the whole 640 acres. That was about a year ago. What he offered was about what other land holders was gett'n but those of us who really value what we can do for the kids didn't want the property all screwed up by a bunch of wells on the place. The preacher who was administrator at the time told Phelps we wouldn't lease any minerals. If he had been interested in coal, hell, Jake, the whole ranch would wind up being one big hole in the ground. That's how coal mining is today. They call it open pit and that's about what it is."

"Did this Phelps accept that answer?" Sorrells asked, assuming he hadn't.

"Naw, Jake, he didn't. He tried to go around us and deal with the whole Baptist church and he convinced some of them people what he wanted to do would pay off real well."

"What happened then, Buck?"

"Me and some folks in Century got up a petition asking the church to not do anything that would hurt the Boys Ranch regardless of what it paid. It didn't take much to get the big shots in the church to vote it down. That's when Phelps decided to play rough. First he started buying some politicians and a few guys in the welfare department who he asked to start the idea that the state could do a better job raising our boys than we could. Talk is, he's got a judge, too. Then he brought in a couple of goons to scare our local supporters off. That's when they worked me over.

"Jake, there was something about what you said about solving other folks' problems that sorta indicated to me you might know how to handle this kind'a situation. If I was wrong, just tell me."

Sorrells looked at the man who had been so important to him as a kid. He reached out to put his hand on Buck's shoulder. "I'm your man," he said.

It would be a fifty-mile drive to Century, a town located in the Tea Pot Dome area, and half the day was already gone. Sorrells gathered up the few items he had unpacked and put them back into his duffel bag. "Let's go to Century, Buck."

Sorrells paid for the room, then paid for another week. "I'll have to let you know if I'm staying longer," he told the clerk. Then he followed Buck to his pickup and they finished their previous conversation. By the time they were nearing Century, Sorrells had a good idea of how he needed to approach the problem.

"Buck, you and me are not going to be seen together. Nobody else should know who I am or why I'm here. That's for your benefit and mine too. I'm going to need some kind of transportation. Who do you know that you can trust to keep their mouth shut?"

"Jake," Buck grinned, "hell, I got kinfolk all over this country." As if to prove his point, Buck pulled up beside a two-pump gas station in a small town about fifteen miles from Century. "This here is my nephew's place," he told Sorrells. "He's always got some kinda extra cars around."

The nephew looked a lot like his uncle, the same lean frame. Buck didn't bother with introductions. "This here's an old friend of mine. He's in the market for some kind of dependable transportation."

"Buck," the nephew asked, "how you gettin' along? I heard some guys liked to beat you to death."

THE GERMAN WOMAN'S HIRED HAND

"They did their damndest. I guess I was just too ornery to die."

The nephew looked Sorrells over, then said, "I ain't got much on hand, but you're welcome to take a look."

Behind the station there was a garage bay that was used primarily to put tires on cars and do other service work. Behind that were a few older model cars, one of which was a rundown prewar Dodge panel wagon. One fender was dented and almost all its paint faded till there was no discernable color remaining.

"Does that one run?" Sorrells asked.

"Oh yeah, it runs, the battery is down now, but it will hold a charge. Some guy brought it in almost six months ago. Wanted the motor overhauled. I done the work but the SOB never came back. Is that thing something you'd be interested in? My repairs run near a hundred bucks and I had to put some better tires on it. Guess a couple of hundred would do, but ain't you look'n for something better?"

A grin came to Sorrells face. "I'm not used to much. You should see what I'm driving now. Does it have a heater? This Wyoming wind is freezing me to death."

"Yeah, hell, everything in this country's got a heater," the nephew answered.

There was a look exchanged between the uncle and his nephew, then the younger man turned to Sorrells. "You being here got anything to do with what happened to Uncle Buck?"

Sorrells made no response.

"Mister, if it does, you can take the damn Dodge. Bring it back or not as long as them bastards get paid back for what they done to Buck."

"I'll try to get it back in one piece," said Jake, "and thanks, but you never saw me with Buck!"

While they waited for the battery to charge, the two men went to a small café to have a cup of coffee and eat a sandwich. When they returned, the Dodge was being filled with gas and had the windows wiped till at least it was possible to see through them. "Let me pay you for the gas," Sorrells said.

"No sir. This here's a family thing."

Sorrells nodded. "Yeah, for me too."

The heater was working, but had trouble heating the cavernous inside of the panel wagon. In addition, the thing was geared so low it could barely reach fifty miles an hour. Sorrells didn't care ... he didn't own it anyway, but the heavy Mackinaw coat he was wearing was hard pressed to keep him warm. It was dark when he followed Buck's pickup onto the grounds of the Baptist Boys Ranch. There were a number of simple cottages that housed married staff, and Buck still lived in the one he was in when Sorrells was at the ranch. His wife had died two years earlier and his two daughters were grown and married. Both had been beautiful dark haired girls about Sorrells' age. Their mother was a full blood Cheyenne and the girls bore the evidence of their heritage. Jake Sorrells had been the only boy on the ranch that Buck had trusted with his daughters.

They parked the Dodge behind the house out of easy sight. Both Sorrells and Buck were tired so it was early to bed, but not until Sorrells knew everything Buck knew about the man who was so openly seeking to take control of the property.

The next morning after Sorrells and Buck had their coffee, they went to the barn. Since Buck's stay in the hospital, several of the ranch's older boys had been trying to fill in. Buck had introduced Sorrells simply as an old friend.

"They mean well," Buck told Sorrells later, "but they ain't nothing like you was when it comes to take'n on tough jobs."

"Just let them be kids, Buck. This place is likely to be the best thing they'll ever know."

Buck wasn't officially back to work, so there was time during the afternoon for them to drive around Century so Sorrells could re-orient himself to the city. There was a new place at the end of the city limits that Buck pointed out as a sometimes hangout for the two thugs that had attacked him. It was a sort of roadhouse that sat in a clump of tall pines. Sorrells made note that there was no obvious outdoor lighting.

"How often you think the guys come here?" he asked.

"When they're in town, pretty near ever night," Buck said.

It was a pattern, and in Sorrells' work, patterns of behavior were important. They were driving the old panel wagon and Sorrells pulled up at the edge of the gravel parking lot and sat taking in every detail of the property. His mind was already focused on the job ahead. After a few minutes, he started the engine and turned to Buck.

"Show me this place where Phelps has his office."

That location received even more scrutiny than the roadhouse. It was a rustic older house that Phelps not only used as his local office, but was a place to stay when he was in the area. It was set back in the woods and could only be accessed by a single driveway. Later that night, Sorrells would return alone to make a closer reconnaissance.

Any plans Sorrells had would be carried out at night, and the Wyoming nights were in the ten degree range with sometimes howling winds of near thirty to forty miles an hour. To Sorrells, that was good, for it would help to mask sounds. When he returned to the Ranch, Buck was waiting up with a pot of coffee. Once he had warmed himself, he lit a cigarette and shocked Buck by asking, "Do you still keep a few sticks of dynamite around to clear stumps?"

"Yeah, I do, but why you ask'n?"

"That's another thing you don't want to know. There's something else you used to keep, some kind of shotgun. Is that still here?"

"It sure is, but a couple of years ago I cut the barrels down, so it ain't any good for hunt'n."

"That depends on what you're hunting. Sometime tomorrow, why don't you get two or three sticks of dynamite and find that shotgun and whatever shells you've got. I'm planning on needing them."

"Jake, what the hell kind'a work do you do?"

Sorrells looked into Buck's eyes and grinned. "I'm currently a hired hand on a ranch in Oklahoma!"

"Damn it, boy! You must be one hell of a hand!"

"I do my best," Sorrells replied.

The next day he drove to town. It was almost Christmas and every storefront had been decorated. In a few places colored lights stretched across the main street. Everywhere, Sorrells saw people shopping, and that reminded him that for the first time in his life, he needed to purchase gifts. He saw a hardware store, went in and bought two pocket knives, a Case with a mother-of-pearl handle for Buck and one that had a lot of strange looking blades, all practically useless, but the kind of thing a kid like Charlie would like. The clerk that waited on him called it a Swiss something. It had a red handle.

Sorrells felt at ease in a hardware store. His next stop would prove more complicated. He stood staring at display cases, all offering a wide choice of pretty items. A smiling sales lady offered her assistance, realizing that he was in distress. She knew most men were, especially in a jewelry store.

"Perhaps a nice ring?" she suggested.

"No, don't think so." Sorrells moved away to another display case.

"Is this for your wife?" she asked. Sorrells simply shook his head.

"A girlfriend?"

"No ma'am." Sorrells was relieved when she led him to a display of gold chains. He eagerly bought the first one she extracted from the case. She suggested adding a gold cross and Sorrells liked the idea.

"Would you like it wrapped?"

"I'd be obliged," he said as he pulled enough cash from his pocket to cover the expense. He told himself he would never again put foot in another jewelry store, Christmas or not! One good thing though, his purchases would easily fit into his duffel bag.

Jake's absence had required Helga and Charlie to make some adjustments. By silent agreement, they never spoke of him. Somehow they instinctively knew his absence would be easier to bear if they didn't, and all went well for the most part.

They set up the Christmas tree in the little-used living room and spent pleasant evenings there in its flickering lights, reading, listening to music and munching the peanut brittle Charlie had mastered so well that Helga felt some concern for his teeth. Electric candles flickered in the windows, and Pup curled up on the braided rug in front of the fireplace until Charlie whistled him to bed in the guest room where he had agreed to sleep throughout the duration.

When Elsie Mason suggested the Dibs seamstresses were drowning in local orders and could use a break, Helga declared a vacation in their behalf. "You have families of your own," she said. "Go home. Enjoy the holidays. These are gift certificates," she continued as she handed out the cleverly designed cards. "Sell them for ten percent less than the amount of your customers' orders and assure them you'll do your best to get their purchases to them after the first of the year."

As for the void Jake had left them in manpower, Charlie welcomed Helga's help with chores throughout the mornings and most evenings, and mid-days they might shop in Woodson for last minute gifts to wrap secretively that night and hide among the growing accumulation beneath the tree. Or they might drink spiced punch with Melba and her jolly customers beneath the red and green lights that rimmed the cafe's windows. One day they delivered Christmas baskets of Helga's homemade cookies and plum jam to their neighbors, and always Charlie's peanut brittle.

Chapter Fifteen
Buck Thomas

The day after Jake's shopping spree, he put Buck in the back of the Dodge where he could not be seen and they waited across the street from a café where Phelps and his "assistants" often met for lunch. Phelps was the first to arrive. He was a fifty-something man who wore an overcoat and a western-style dress cowboy hat. He moved briskly to the café, holding the brim of his hat against the cold wind. A few minutes later a maroon Oldsmobile parked just down the street and a pair of men, both burly and tough looking, emerged and proceeded to the café.

"That's them!" Buck said, his hand pointing across the seat.

That night Sorrells revisited the roadhouse, waited an hour, but saw no trace of the maroon Olds. He then drove by the house occupied by Phelps. He could see lights on, but before he made his move, he would need to deal with his two goons. He drove back to Buck's place.

Sorrells hoped to have this matter resolved and be back at the Marston Ranch for the holidays. He would need to get lucky to make it by then. On the fourth night of his stay, he found the Oldsmobile parked in the roadhouse parking lot. Then he drove to check on the Phelps residence. Once again he saw lights burning. He would need to move quickly, but in similar situations he had always moved with dispatch.

It was after ten when Sorrells arrived back at the roadhouse. The crowd inside was celebrating the season just as he had always done, by drinking. Sorrells edged up beside the Oldsmobile, then pushed the Dodge bumper into the rear quarter panel, just enough to cause a substantial dent but not disable the car. Its owners would need to get out of town later. He left the bumper of the Dodge lodged in the Oldsmobile's side and pulled Buck's sawed-off shotgun from under the seat. Just before he stepped into the bar, he leaned the gun against a bush out of the light, but easily available. Then he went inside, found a bartender and asked him if he knew the man who owned the car he had just struck.

The bartender looked at Sorrells with a smile. "I know 'em," he said, "but was I you, I'd use this time to get out'ta here. Those guys are mean as hell and half drunk besides."

"No sir," Sorrells replied, purposely slurring his words, "I'm a little tight myself, but I want'a pay for what I did."

"You will," the bartender said as he stepped over to the table where the thugs were entertaining two ladies. Sorrells saw the bartender point him out and the two men rise from their chairs.

"You the bastard that hit our car?" one demanded.

"Yes sir, I am, but I intend to do the right thing."

The two men pushed Sorrells towards the door. For a minute they stood staring at the side of their car, the beat up Dodge still buried in the shiny paint. Then, with menacing expressions, they turned to Sorrells, who by now had the shotgun pointed at their knees.

"You boys are going to need some vocational training for your new occupation," he said as both barrels exploded and the widely spread shot took the legs out from beneath the two men who had beaten Buck Thomas. "You aren't going to die, but you'll never threaten decent folks again," growled Sorrells.

Sorrells climbed into his truck and backed away just as the crowd came rushing from the bar to see what the shooting was about. He drove directly to Phelps' place, only this time he turned into the driveway. He checked to see that his .45 Colt was still in the pocket of his Mackinaw, then walked to the door and pounded on it as he called out, "Mr. Phelps! Mr. Phelps!"

It took a couple of minutes before he heard a voice yell back, "Who are you and what do you want?"

"It's a couple of friends of yours, they been hurt, hurt real bad!" Sorrells made his voice sound overly excited.

The door opened a crack, "What the hell you mean, hurt?" Sorrells kicked the door open and pushed inside, Colt in hand.

"What is this?" Phelps had not gotten to this point in his life by being meek. His face was defiant.

"I'm here to help you pack," Sorrells said. "Let's start with what cash you got stashed around."

"I don't have any cash here. What are you, some kind of cheap thief?"

"I'm here to tell you to leave Century; to leave the state of Wyoming, and most of all to leave the Boys Ranch alone."

"You some sort of preacher? Some kind of religious nut?"

"You can consider me an avenging angel if you like," Sorrells said softly, "but I do things other angels can't do. Like shoot your worthless ass!"

Phelps raised his hands and shook them in a mocking manner, "I'm scared," he laughed.

The force of the .45 slug as it passed through the palm of Phelps' hand knocked him down. When he rose he was gripping his wrist, staring at the blood pumping from his wound.

"You shot me, you crazy bastard!" he screamed.

Sorrells pulled a bandana from his rear pocket and threw it on the top of Phelps' desk. "You better wrap that up. Make it tight. A man could bleed to death," Sorrells' said.

"I need to get to the hospital," Phelps pleaded.

"You're right about that, but before you do, I want you to get in that desk and pull out all the cash."

"I told you, I don't have any cash!" There was little defiance in his tone now. It was more emotional.

"Sure you do." Sorrells grinned. "Men like you always have enough around to pay off their political friends. I'm sure you don't write personal checks. You don't pay goons by check either. Why don't you do yourself a favor and just lay it here on your desk?"

Frantically, Phelps reached for his keys to unlock one of the desk drawers and withdrew a canvas bank bag. Sorrells opened it. As he suspected, it was filled with hundred dollar bills.

"Take the damn money and leave," Phelps cried, "I got'ta get to the hospital!"

Sorrells stepped up and placed the nose of his pistol against the bridge of Phelps' nose. "If I hear of you anywhere near the Baptist Boys Ranch again or doing anything to cause them any problem, I'll come wherever you are and send your worthless ass straight to hell! Do you understand?"

"Anything you say," he moaned. "You can't argue with a mad man."

"Then go!"

Phelps, grasping his bleeding hand, rushed out of the house to his car. Sorrells reached into his inside pocket and pulled out a stick of dynamite, the fuse already in place. He lit the fuse with his Zippo lighter and threw the dynamite on the floor. Then he reached down and scooped up the bag of cash and walked out of the house. He had just pulled away when the house exploded behind him. He then drove back for one more visit with Buck before he left Wyoming.

There was still a light on in Buck's house. Sorrells knew there would be. It was as if the father he'd never had was waiting up for the return of his prodigal son. When Sorrells opened the door, neither man spoke. They said it all with their eyes. Finally Buck said, "Is it over?"

"It's over," Sorrells replied as he set the bag of cash on Buck's kitchen table.

"What's that?" Buck asked.

Sorrells reached down, unzipped the opening and dumped an unimaginable amount of hundred dollar bills across the table.

"My God Almighty!" Buck exclaimed. "What the hell is that?"

Sorrells went over to refill Buck's coffee cup and pour one for himself. Still without speaking, he reached down to draw twenty bills from the pile. He pushed half of them over to Buck, then slipped the other ten into his pocket. "This is my expense money," he said, "and what you have there should take care of your hospital bills."

"What's the rest for?" Buck asked.

"You're going to take it and see that every boy here at the ranch gets a really good Christmas present. How you handle that is up to you. Say the money comes from a benefactor who wants to remain anonymous."

"My bill at the hospital ain't near this big," Buck offered.

"Neither are my expenses. "But what the hell, it's Christmas. Any extra money — and there ought to be a lot — give it to the Ranch. Now listen to me, Buck. I've been in deals like this before and you haven't. I need you to call your nephew and tell him I'm bringing his Dodge back tonight. See if you can talk him into taking me back to Casper."

"Hell, boy, I'll be glad to take you!"

"No. You stay here. I don't want you involved." Sorrells set his cup down and rose from his chair. "I'm leaving now. I'll leave your shotgun with your nephew."

"He'll be wait'n for you, Jake. You can count on that."

Sorrells checked his watch. It was almost one o'clock. He had packed his duffel bag that morning, but to its contents he added the new cash and the .45.

"Call your nephew, Buck. Tell him I'll be there in less than an hour. Oh, I forgot something!" Sorrells reached into his pocket and pulled out the knife he'd bought at the hardware store. "Merry Christmas, Buck." His arm reached around Buck's shoulders.

"God bless you, Jake. Take care of yourself."

"I'll try," Sorrells said with a grin.

In the first few days of Jake's absence, Mary had called to say the church board had met to discuss Howard Sinclair's harsh treatment of the middle school students, who paid half a dollar (for supplies, he said) to attend his evening photography workshop in the church basement. After hearing first-hand accounts of his physically jerking the children around, of his impatience and general rudeness, the church board voted to censure him and send him on his way, but the women's groups banded together in favor of addressing his evil nature with huge doses of their motherly love instead.

Helga was gasping by the time Mary asked her to pray that Howard's heart be touched. She had been on the verge of telling poor sweet, gullible Mary that Howard had called her repeatedly in the last week, flattering her with false praise and showering her with sympathy that one so deserving as she should have to endure life sequestered on a farm.

Howard's idiocy had been amusing to both Helga and Charlie the first time or two, but it got old very quickly, and Helga had alerted Betsy, the switchboard operator, to the situation. Once she had learned to recognize Howard's voice, she intercepted his calls, telling him the party phone line was busy, or the lines were down, or the phone was out of order, and Helga just let the phone ring on Betsy's day off.

It was nearly dawn when Buck's nephew dropped Sorrells off in front of his hotel. Too early to get a drink, the way he would customarily unwind after one of his jobs had ended. He would need to settle for however long he could sleep.

The notion that he ought to be drunk had not left since he'd climbed out of bed at ten that morning. He could get some breakfast, and by then the bars would be open. All this was in his mind, but for the first time there was some sort of contradictory force. One he could not comprehend.

For Charlie, the most outstanding event of the season so far had been hands down the all-school Christmas program where he and Jennie Lou Carter, a.k.a. Christmas angel, stood on either side of the punch bowl making eyes at each other for half an hour following the production before her parents took her home. That was the first night since Jake left that Charlie hadn't fallen asleep with thoughts of him on his mind.

Sleep was never easy for Helga, and it was especially hard to come by the night of the Christmas program. Several of the parents had asked about Jake. She had told them he was out of state visiting relatives but would be back by Christmas, and she fervently hoped she hadn't lied. In all other ways, life went on comfortably at the Marston Ranch, Helga layering tradition after tradition upon Charlie's first ever Christmas, experiencing the holiday anew through his eyes, loving him into the child of her heart.

Jake checked out of the hotel, but instead of a bar, the force pulled him to the train station to start the first leg of his journey. If the trains and buses had been a problem before, now, filled with people traveling for the holiday made matters even worse. It was worse yet when he rode the bus. At every stop, and there were many, Sorrells had the feeling he could simply get off and celebrate Christmas, in the way he had always done, by going on a weeklong binge. But he didn't. The trip to Casper had taken two and a half days. The return trip took longer, the transfer connections often missed. He sat staring at men who prepared for their journeys by bringing brown paper sacks that Sorrells knew to hold what he wanted more than anything else. He could walk any direction and cure the ache in his gut, but he didn't.

His sleep throughout the trip from Wyoming had come in a series of short naps. In one of them, an old theme came rushing back. Sorrells felt himself falling through air. Otherwise there was no sensation. It was only when he hit the cold water that he noticed the burning feeling in his chest. Instinct made him struggle to reach the surface and breathe. Somehow, he managed to reach the bank, and with great effort pull his body half way out of the cold water. He lay there in the mud, his body growing cold. He felt his soul leaving his body, and his screams shocked his fellow passengers seated around him, staring as he shook himself awake.

When Sorrells stood to exit the bus at his next connection, the man behind him reached up to touch Jake's sleeve. "You going home for Christmas?" he asked. Sorrells looked down, nodded and smiled, but made no reply.

There was no way he could expect to understand, but like all the other travelers who crowded the bus stations in that holiday season, he shared a common pull, in Sorrells' case, unconsciously. He was being drawn home. There had been no other such experience in his entire life and he didn't understand any part of it. It was the 23rd of December 1951, and Jake Sorrells was halfway home.

The bus pulled into Woodson two hours late, just before dusk on Christmas Eve. Jake dug a nickel out of his jeans pocket, found an empty phone booth, and dialed the Lutheran Church parsonage. Mary picked up, music blaring in the background. He identified himself, but before he could ask if the town had a cab service that would take him to Dibs, she was off and running.

"Oh Jake!" she all but shouted, "we were hoping you'd be back for Christmas. Eli's tied up at the church, but Postmaster Sinclair is here picking up a fruitcake I made for Helga. He was going your way to deliver his own gift to Helga anyway, and I know he'd be happy for you to ride along."

Without waiting for a response, she turned to the postmaster. "Wouldn't you, Howard, be happy for Mr. Sorrells to ride along with you to the Marston Ranch?"

Jake heard mumbling but not Howard's response, and then Mary was back on the line saying brightly, "You stay right there, Jake. He'll be on his way once I get the cake packed up and into his car." Then, before Jake could voice an objection, "Merry Christmas," she shouted into the phone, "and welcome home."

He stood there listening to the hum of the dead phone until a woman outside the booth knocked on the glass and raised her eyebrows in a questioning way. He vacated the booth apologetically and was standing outside the bus station smoking his third cigarette when the postmaster pulled up to the curb, rolled down the window, stuck his head out, and hollered from the curb:

"Looks like the weather's going to get bad," he called out. "I wouldn't want to get caught out in it, what with no tire chains and all. Get your gear and I'll take you as far as the highway. Maybe you can hitch a ride on into Dibs. It shouldn't be a problem for an outdoorsy hired hand like yourself to make it on to the Marston Ranch from there. You could probably fit Mrs. Steigner's cake into your duffel bag and take it along too."

Jake hadn't moved from where he leaned against the bus building. Now he ground out his cigarette and, leaving his gear where it lay, he made his way to the curb where Howard sat smirking beyond the open window of his car. Jake figured he was close enough to say what he had on his mind without disturbing the peace, but before he got started, Ed Mason pulled his truck up behind the parked car.

"Jake," he called out, "is that you? What the hell are you doing in Woodson on Christmas Eve? Get your stuff and pile it in the back, and we'll get on home."

Jake acknowledged Ed with a nod, then wrenched the postmaster's door wide open, grabbed up Mary's cake with his left hand and said, "Merry Christmas, you son of a bitch," before his right fist connected solidly with the postmaster's jaw. "That was for Charlie," Jake all but whispered before closing the door softly.

He transferred his duffel bag to Ed's truck and, after a while, allowed that he'd had business up north. Ed shifted gears and allowed that he'd delivered a load of feed to an idiot rancher the other side of Woodson who hadn't had the sense to stock up until now. Other than that, although Ed had seen the action that transpired at the curb, and though he wondered what sort of business had inspired Jake to take a bus anywhere, and though he wondered what in hell Jake was doing with a fruitcake in his lap, the trip to the Marston Ranch passed in silence, small talk not being necessary between them.

Helga in a green satin dress she had made and Charlie wearing the red Christmas shirt she had also made, arrived at the dining room door together. Pup was there too, but he had rejected his red and green plaid Christmas collar early on, and Charlie had hung it on the tree. Helga opened the dining room door and lo and behold, Howard Sinclair himself would have been impressed by the long dining room table covered in fine linen, the flickering of tall white candles reflected in gleaming silver and crystal, and a veritable banquet laid out on the table where three place settings waited to be claimed.

They had taken their seats at the table when Charlie heard Mason's truck come to a stop out front and he was out the door in a flash with Pup at his heels. Helga's heart raced and she yearned to race too, but she remained where she sat, listening to a truck door slam followed by Jake's voice in the kitchen where he was depositing Mary's fruitcake.

When she thought she could control her voice, she called out, "Merry Christmas and welcome home! Get washed up and come to the table before the turkey dries out," and then there he was in the doorway, travel weary but a puzzled grin making its way across his face.

"What's all this?" he said, waving his hand about. "and why haven't we eaten in here before?"

"There's never been an occasion worthy until now," said Helga as she made her way around the table to embrace him. "Merry Christmas," she whispered, "and welcome home. We've missed you."

He shoved his duffel bag under the table where the gifts he'd brought would be handy, and Christmas fell into place for Jake Sorrells in that instant.

The blizzard Sinclair had predicted earlier arrived late Christmas Eve. All of Woodson County was iced in until New Year's Day, when Howard Sinclair's car was pulled out of a snow bank east of Dibs. The postmaster's lifeless body was draped over the steering wheel.

On the seat beside him in a canvas bag marked United States Postal Service was the cash that had gone missing the day before Christmas. It lay beside a Woodson Lutheran Church bank deposit bag containing the church's Christmas Eve Services' benevolent funds offering.

The women's groups were furious, but the preacher's wife grieved and could not be comforted. There was no accounting for the postmaster's broken jaw, but enough speculation to keep the party lines ringing throughout New Year's Day

Chapter Sixteen
Les Jones

The blizzard had blasted its way south and in less than a week Dibs' roads turned to slush bordered by diminishing drifts. Les Jones plodded through stockyard muck, prodding reluctant cattle onto trucks waiting to take them to slaughter. Les was lonely. It had been a long time since he was welcome at Clem's Café, and other doors had closed to him more recently.

He had given Melba reason to hate him even before Sorrells had ripped the whip from his hand in defense of Charlie. Now even the locals he had considered his friends avoided him. They too had settled differences with hired help, but they wouldn't think of using a whip on a fifteen-year-old boy. He was a shunned man, and that was the Marston hand's fault. Each passing day, he became more determined to settle the score. One day, thought Les. One day soon.

While he waited for the time to be right, he sat alone in the filthy room the stockyard provided its employee, dodging drips from the leaking roof, consuming the alcohol that fueled his hatred for Jake Sorrells, for the boy who had caused the trouble, and for Melba McCord.

Everywhere he'd gone since the day Sorrells blindsided him in the ramp, someone had made a smart-ass remark. That damn Melba kept feeding the fire, but his old pool hall buddies weren't much better.

He had to get out of this stinkin' town, but first he would settle some scores, starting with that damn waitress who had turned him down years ago. Then Sorrells and the kid. They started it. And maybe the German woman, too.

"I'll be long gone, but I'll leave 'em something to remember me by. You can bet on that." He threw the bottle against the wall of the shack, pulled on his greasy windbreaker, and lurched out into the night. Les Jones had had enough.

Melba cleared the dishes from the last customers' booth and rubbed the table dry with a towel. Her dad had finished cleaning the kitchen and headed for the house, maybe a hundred feet behind the café. A convenient arrangement, considering the hours they worked. Except for the beer joint at the edge of town, the café was generally the last business to close. She glanced at the wall clock and reached for her Mackinaw. It was late. Time for her to get on home. The sidewalks, where they existed, were deserted. The only traffic on Main Street was the occasional truck passing through.

The wind had picked up, but Melba found it refreshing after being cooped up all afternoon. She chose her steps carefully through the slush. The town didn't have streetlights, though several of the bigger towns in the county did. What passed for Dibs's city council would occasionally bring up the need at one of their meetings, but there had never been enough interest to merit the expense. Clem McCord would have cause to encourage them to reconsider the topic at their next meeting.

When she passed a dark vacant lot, she noticed a pickup parked along a bare patch where a sidewalk should have been. She squinted into the dark, thinking she knew whose truck it was, but Les was nowhere in sight. If it's his, she thought, he probably got drunk and left it there.

Melba was no more than two steps beyond the pickup when Les stepped out of the darkness and hit her with his fist. Later, she would say she remembered nothing until she found herself on the floorboard of his pickup as it sped out of town. She tried to pull herself up, but he pulled the truck to the side of the road and struck her until she was unconscious.

He turned off the blacktop onto the road leading past the Marston Ranch and proceeded three miles beyond, slipping and sliding on the waterlogged road to an abandoned farmhouse, where he pulled Melba out of the truck and onto the sagging porch. She revived, realized his intentions, and managed to mumble, "No, Les, no! It's not worth it," but he continued the onslaught, beating and kicking her into senselessness and still wasn't satisfied.

Mercifully, she hadn't regained consciousness when he raped her and then looked down at the tangled flesh that was Melba McCord and laughed. The bitch deserved what she'd gotten and more. He had a sawed off .12 gauge behind the pickup seat, but chances were good she was already dead. I'll save my ammunition for Sorrells, he thought. Him and that damn kid he took back to the Marston Ranch with him.

In the bungalow behind the café, Clem had grown uneasy when he woke in his easy chair to the realization that his daughter wasn't home yet. From the bedroom window, he saw that the lights were off in the café, and his alarm heightened. He grabbed up a flashlight and went outside to walk the familiar path between the two buildings. His mouth dry and his heart racing, he sounded the alarm when the beam of his flashlight settled on the purse that had fallen from Melba's shoulder. She was somewhere out there, alone and vulnerable, and he was helpless to save her.

Within the hour, every grown man and boy in the Dibs vicinity had responded to Clem's alarm and turned out with torches, flashlights and various weapons. They broke up into teams and headed out in all directions while their wives and daughters brewed coffee in the basement of the church and waited. Team by team, they returned to the church where they downed hot coffee, pulled on the dry clothes their womenfolk had brought from home and set out again.

Melba wasn't found until early the next morning when a farmer who leased the land from an absentee landlord dropped by the property to check for flooding following the thaw.

"I thought she was dead," he told Deputy Strange, " but then I heard her moan, so I wrapped her in a blanket the wife keeps in the truck and brung her on into town as fast as the roads would allow.

"Never even knew who she was till now. You know," he paused to scratch his head, then added, "I reckon I've seen Melba every work'n day for the last ten years. She was so damn beat up I never recognized her."

If Deputy Roy Strange had thought he knew what it was to hate, he redefined that emotion the moment he laid eyes on the ruined figure of the woman he hadn't known until then that he loved. Melba would live. He would will her to live. And the man who had done this would pay. Oh, yes, he would pay.

Reality set in by degrees after Les sobered up. He had left Melba for dead, but whether or not she survived, he would have to get out of town. But not too far or for too long. He hadn't finished with Sorrells and the kid. He'd been lucky with Melba. With Sorrells, he would need more than luck.

He left the stockyard shack for the second time that night, this time with all he owned, including blankets, enough canned goods to tide him over, half a dozen jugs of rotgut he'd buried beneath the floor, and a box of shells for the sawed-off shotgun. There was a place maybe twenty miles south of Dibs in cave country where he could hole up for a couple of days, but he'd be back. Les wasn't one to leave a job unfinished once he'd made up his mind.

On party lines, in kitchens over coffee, down at the feed store, over cue sticks at the pool hall and beers at the domino parlor, the question on everyone's lips was, "Who could have done this to Melba?" As far as anyone knew, she didn't have an enemy in the world. That mess between her and Jones blew over almost as soon as it began. Besides, that was years ago. He spouted off plenty after she turned him away from the café last spring, but he gave that up when his cronies stopped listening.

Clem returned from the hospital the next morning, hung a CLOSED sign on the door of his business, and drove back to Woodson, prepared to stay until he could bring Melba home with him. A cloud of grief hung over the diehards who congregated beneath the café's tattered awning. Some sat on familiar wooden benches, others stood, their hands deep in the bibs of their overalls, or hunkered down on what passed for a curb. They could get coffee at home, but there hadn't been a day in the past ten years when Melba's cheerful banter hadn't started their day on a hopeful note. Whoever did this was going to pay, and it wasn't long before they knew who that scum was.

Smithers from down at the stockyard sent up the alarm when Jones didn't show that morning, and suddenly, for once in his life, he was somebody. There wasn't a soul in all of Dibs who didn't hang on Smithers' every word, though they didn't amount to more than, "Les Jones cleared out in the night and took everything he owns with him."

Melba confirmed their speculations when word got back from the hospital that she had waked screaming the name of her attacker. Roy Strange checked the ammunition in his revolver, set up a chair outside her hospital room, and waited.

Surprisingly, hours later she woke almost cheerful, asking when she would be released to go home. The nurses weren't fooled. Melba was coping out of consideration for the people she loved. They had seen it before. Her father had been beside himself with anger and grief, but his daughter was awake now. The stitches would come out in a couple of weeks and her hair would grow back in no time. She was going to be just fine. And if she wasn't, no one but Melba would know.

Clem returned to the cafe, made an urn of coffee, and hung the OPEN sign on the door. Melba would be home soon and things would get back to normal. Only she knew the depth of the scars that would never heal, but she would keep those to herself.

Sadie Dale, alias Clarissa Fontaine, had borne such scars since long before she and Melba boarded the bus headed for a California abortion clinic her aunt had chosen. Old man Dale drowned in his own vomit shortly thereafter. Clarissa didn't attend the funeral. Now, these many years later, she walked into Melba's hospital room with an armful of roses. She didn't stay long and they didn't talk. Just held each other and knew. It was better that way.

Helga, too, knew the depth of such scars. She sat long hours beside Melba's bed while Deputy Strange maintained his post outside her room.

Chapter Seventeen
Hell Breaks Loose

Melba was still recuperating in the hospital two days later when Jones made his move. Holing up in the caves south of Dibs hadn't improved his disposition or softened his convictions. Sorrells and the kid had to die, and the German woman if she got in his way.

He checked his pockets for his keys before shuffling out of the cave, leaving it littered with empty cans and several empty rotgut jugs, his only comfort throughout the time he'd been hidden away in that godforsaken place.

He hauled himself up into the cab of the truck, hawked and spat out the window, wiped the back of his hand across his mouth and headed out toward the Marston Ranch. It was well after midnight, a good time to pay a final visit to Sorrells. The kid would be easy after he disposed of him.

Jones had hung around with John Marston. He'd been to the ranch several times before Marston went missing, so he knew the layout. Unless Sorrells and the German woman had worked out a better arrangement, he and the kid would be asleep in the bunkhouse. That would be where to start. He reached down in the seat for a pack of Camels, worked one out of the pack and lit it with a kitchen match. As the smoke wafted out the open window, he thought through various details, snickering to himself. He knew exactly how he would kill Sorrells.

Les parked his pickup about a hundred yards from the ranch headquarters. He pushed the seat up and pulled out his shotgun, then filled his coat pocket with as many .12 gauge shells as he could cram inside.

He saw that there were no lighted windows on the property. Good. He would have the advantage of surprise. He rested the shotgun against the lot fence and dragged two bales of hay from the barn to the bunkhouse. A howling Oklahoma wind had started up on the heels of the thawing, and it and the sun had done him a favor. The wood plank bunkhouse would light up like a tinderbox.

He detected no movement inside the bunkhouse when he looked through a darkened window. As quietly as possible, he broke open the two hay bales, piling the loose hay against the side of the bunkhouse. He struck matches several times before flames flew up from the hay. In the light of the fire as it spread up the dry wood walls, he retrieved his shotgun and took position beside the open barn door, down on one knee, with a fist full of shotgun shells spread out on the ground in front of him.

A dog barked inside the bunkhouse. The kid was in there, all right, and Sorrells, too. The mutt's barking would wake them. They'd be confused, choking on smoke and bleary-eyed when they ran out of the burning bunkhouse, and his shotgun would find them within range. Easy, he thought. He would pick them off one at a time. Things were working out. He hoped the kid would come out first so Sorrells would see him die.

Jones had made only one error in his calculations, but it would seriously complicate his plans. Sorrells had not moved back into the bunkhouse. The change in his relationship with Helga had kept him with her in the house.

That night, they lay in each other's arms as they had almost every night since he had been sober. A faint sound roused him. Pup was yapping, had been yapping for some time, and Charlie would never allow that to go on. Something was wrong. Jake worked free of the legs that had entwined with his, pulled on his jeans and boots and felt his way through the dark to the door. The blast of Les's shotgun rang out as he stepped onto the porch. From the light of the burning bunkhouse, he saw the outline of two figures. One of them was on the ground.

He thought there might be a gun in the house, but he didn't have time to search for it. By then, Helga was beside him. "Phone for help," he said as he reached into the kitchen drawer, came away with Helga's sharpest knife and headed for the door.

"That won't do it!" she called after him, frantically twisting the crank that would bring the operator on line. Betsy was on duty that night, and Helga was grateful. Not all the area operators were as level headed as they might be, but Betsy was. "We need help," Helga hollered into the phone.

"Someone's shot and down in the yard, and it has to be Charlie. Jake's gone out after whoever shot him. The bunkhouse is on fire. Whoever's got the fastest car in Dibs, tell them to get out here. We need to get Charlie to the Woodson hospital the minute we can get to him. Call them. Tell them we're coming."

Betsy did better than that. Rousing her boyfriend Jim, a mechanic who raced his souped up Chevy hot rod at the edge of town Saturday nights, she directed him to the Marston Ranch, then alerted the fire department and Deputy Strange, thereby spreading the word over every party line in the area. By the time Helga replaced the receiver, Sorrells had jumped off the porch and hit the ground running toward the fire and the figure on the ground. Between threatening though ineffectual growls, Pup continued to bark at the intruder.

Jones had moved a couple of steps toward the bunkhouse, expecting Sorrells to rush out of the flames. Well, he thought, if he wants to burn hisself up, that'll be fine too. Then, out of the corner of his eye, he saw Sorrells running all out in his direction, and in one motion he raised the shotgun and fired. The muzzle flashed fire and Sorrells fell to the ground clutching his leg. At that moment the fire flared up and he knew that Les Jones was the shooter.

He was reloading when Sorrells began dragging himself forward. Jones moved back into the closest shadows available, which happened to be those cast by the poultry house. From his cover, not knowing his target was out of range, Les fired again. Sorrells raised himself to a standing position and, by jolts and jerks, managed to drag Charlie a safer distance away. He could feel a pulse, but he knew the boy's wounds were serious. Jones fired once more, then realized Sorrells was out of range and retreated further into the shadows.

The key! Helga thought. Sorrells' firearms were locked in the barn storage room, and they didn't have a chance without a gun. She combed her mind, trying to remember where he said it was hidden. She jerked open the refrigerator door, located the key in the crisper and ran across the uneven ground to Sorrells. He saw her form silhouetted against the bright light of the fire and yelled out, "Get back to cover!"

"Not on your life!" she yelled back at him, and then the three of them were huddled together on the ground. "It's Charlie," she sobbed. "I knew it was. Is he dead? God, tell me he's not going to die!"

"He's hurt but alive. We can't move him without risking both of us being shot, but we've got to stop the bleeding." Sorrells pulled out his bandana, folded it into a square and pressed it tightly against the wound in Charlie's side. Pup was whining in earnest now, licking Charlie's face.

"Did you reach anybody on the phone?"

"Yes, but it'll take them a while to get here. How bad is your leg wound?"

"I'll live," he said, "it's Charlie I'm worried about."

Sorrells knew time would run out for Charlie if they couldn't move him soon. Helga ripped strips from the skirt of her nightgown and together they tied them tightly about the bandana handkerchief Sorrells had used to pack the wound. Then, before he had time to react, Helga was racing toward the barn, her bare legs flying, intent upon finding the firearms that would allow them a defense.

She had no sooner taken off than Les rounded the poultry house and followed her into the barn. Sorrells tried to warn her, but the fire crackled loudly and she was too far away. Painfully, he dragged himself across the rough terrain, finally pulling himself upright at the barn door and silently entering the darkness.

He heard voices coming from the direction of the storage room and limped toward them. Les, one arm about Helga's throat, snarled dark promises he intended to keep. Sorrells had the knife in his hand as he moved silently forward.

He heard Pup's frantic barking and the sound of the bunkhouse collapsing in a pile of smoking embers. In the flash of light, he saw Helga struggling in Jones' arms and heard him scream out when her knee hit his groin and her nails scraped at his eyes. Still, he didn't relinquish his grasp until Sorrells threw himself through the doorway. Then Jones hit her in the head with the butt of the shotgun and they fell to the ground together in one of the stalls. Les knelt, bracing the shotgun across the rails. "I'm fixin' to blow you to hell, you son-of-a-bitch!" he yelled.

Jake's mind reeled. Charlie was down, Helga lay bleeding, and this was the man who was responsible.

"I've killed the kid and I'm gon'na kill you," hollered Jones. Then I figger on finishin' off this German bitch of yours like I done with the other one." He moved cautiously out of the stall and advanced to where he had seen Sorrells stand, clutching a rail, supporting himself upright. He paused, holding his shotgun at waist level, ready to fire at the slightest movement or sound.

If he had listened more closely, he might have heard Sorrells move in behind him. Before the knife slit his throat, what he did hear was Sorrells whisper, "You're in my playground now, you bastard."

Les's eyes dimmed and the light began to fade as Jake stood over him, watching his blood flow out onto the straw-covered barn floor.

Helga dragged herself to the place where his body lay in a heap and then pulled herself upright to look down upon him for maybe a second before she spat in his face. "That's for Melba," she said. Then, turning to Sorrells, "Charlie's waiting. Let's go."

With Helga supporting Jake as best she could, they left Jones to die alone and made their way back to Charlie just as Jim's wildly colorful hot rod streaked into the yard. The whine of Dibs's volunteer fire department's one truck howled in the distance.

Chapter Eighteen
Blood Ties

The ride to the hospital would forever be a blur in Helga's memory. Jake folded his uninjured leg beneath him to make room for his damaged leg in the front seat. Helga scooted into the back seat of Jim's hot rod where she cradled Charlie throughout the half hour race to Woodson, painful memories flooding her mind. She could not, would not, lose Charlie as she had lost her infant son and her brother. The flaming bunkhouse was not a crumbling stone structure. Shotgun blasts were not bombs falling from the sky. No lifeless form had been pulled from the rubble. Blood seeped from Charlie's wound, but his heart beat on.

Attendants waited to receive them at the hospital door. They hurried Charlie off to surgery while others saw to the swelling bump on Helga's head and removed shot pellets from Sorrells' leg, covered the wound with foul smelling ointment and gave him a tetanus shot. He balked at pain meds and refused to be admitted to the hospital, not because he didn't hurt but because he had long ago seen enough of drugs and hospitals to last a lifetime.

Helga wasn't in the waiting area where Sorrells had expected to find her. A crisp, blonde woman at the desk told him Charlie had been dangerously low on blood, but a cross match proved Helga to be the perfect donor. Charlie was still in surgery, and she would need to rest a little longer, but both of them were doing well. Sorrells lowered himself into a plastic chair to wait.

At one point, someone brought him a pair of crutches and tried to demonstrate their use. He accepted the crutches but declined the instructions. "I've used them before," he said. He sat slouched in the chair for what seemed a very long time, one leg of his jeans, torn by the blast of Jones' shot and stiff with dried blood, had been cut away.

Sorrells stretched both legs out in from of him and thought about Helga. He'd known needy women and he'd known self-sufficient women. This one was an interesting mix. For a split second, he wondered if he loved her, but then he fell asleep.

Two hours later, a smiling Helga walked in with the doctor, who reported that Charlie would need time, but he expected a complete recovery and that, yes, they could see him now. Helga and Sorrells spent the few remaining hours of the day in Charlie's room watching him sleep.

By evening, Sorrells had forgone the use of the crutches altogether and, since there was no cafeteria in the hospital and they were both running on caffeine, he and Helga walked and limped to a nearby greasy spoon. They had a long night ahead of them. The two of them would relieve each other beside Charlie's bed while the other tried to get comfortable on the waiting room sofa.

Mary and Eli Steigner arrived the next morning to find them both strangely rested. Charlie was awake and crunching ice, and the worst seemed to be over. He'd been pleased when, at one point in the night, Helga had leaned down to whisper, "We're blood related now, Charlie. Mine's flowing in your veins. But I'm still the boss. When we get back to the ranch, you'll have enough down time to finish reading *Treasure Island*."

"Your hair looks nice," he whispered.

Now what's that all about, she wondered.

"We just this morning heard," said Mary, "or we'd have been here sooner ... Eli had meetings and such, and then there was the wedding. ... I couldn't believe my ears when I turned on the radio this morning. ..."

"There's nothing you could have done," Helga assured her, "but I'm glad you're here now. I was just going in to see Charlie. Would you like to come?"

After the two women left the waiting room, Eli took a seat, turned to Sorrells and asked, "He's dead?"

"Yeah," said Sorrells. "He's dead."

Eli Steigner was a man of God, one who condemned all taking of human life no matter the circumstances. But in his heart he knew Sorrells had done what had to be done. He put his arm across his friend's shoulder and changed the subject. "I believe I have a lead on John Marston," he said. "I'll know more after I make another contact."

"I'll be waiting."

When the women returned, Mary said, "I've been trying to persuade Helga to let us take her back to the ranch, but I'm not making much headway."

Mary's eyebrows shot up to her bangs when Sorrells reached out to trace the bruise darkening on Helga' forehead. "You need to get some sleep," he said. "I'll hold down the fort here." In the end, in spite of Helga's protests, the three of them bundled her up and shuffled her off to the Steigners' car. She was asleep before they passed the Woodson city limits.

Sorrells' second visitor of that day was Deputy Roy Strange. "I've been out to the ranch since first light," he said. "Everything pretty much stacks up like you told me last night. It's just going to be a formality, but with the killing and all, the sheriff wants a full investigation."

"Sure," Sorrells replied, "I understand. Mrs. Marston and I will be glad to cooperate, but you might want to give her a little time.

Things have been happening mighty fast."

"For a lot of us," Strange said. "Melba identified Les Jones as the man who attacked her. Looks like he went plumb crazy. Frankly, I'm glad you killed the bastard. He sure had it coming. In fact, I want to thank you for that. I'm sorry it wasn't me that pulled the trigger, but Helga's knife worked just fine."

"How's Melba doing?" Sorrells asked.

"It's been tough, but she'll mend. She's still here in the hospital if you want to see her. I just came from there. She was awake when I left. Come on. I'll go with you."

Sorrells nodded. "Helga saw her earlier, but she didn't say much. I was on my way up when you walked in."

Melba was sitting in a chair beside the bed when Strange and Sorrells entered her room. Her face was a mass of black and blue bruises and there would doubtless be scars, but the swelling had begun to go down.

She winced and grabbed at her ribs when she turned to greet them, and she mumbled through the stitches in her lips when she spoke. "Helga and Reverend Steigner and his wife were just in to see me," she lisped. The two men moved in closer to hear. "They told me what happened night before last out at the Marston ranch. Thank you, Jake Sorrells. You paid a debt for me that I'll never forget."

"For me, too," said Roy taking her hand, "and I'll damn sure never forget it."

Melba turned slightly toward the deputy and almost managed a smile when she said, "Then you aren't fix'n to cause Sorrells any grief over that?"

"Aw Melba, you know better than that."

"Well, that's good," she said. "I haven't forgot where he got that rotgut whiskey."

Chapter Nineteen
The Late Jake

Helga and Sorrells continued to alternate trips to the hospital until they agreed Jake was better able to see after things at the ranch and she was more adept at nurturing. Helga valued every minute she spent caring for Charlie throughout those two weeks, and he valued the mothering he had never before known. In the end, a bond stronger than the blood they shared had grown between them.

He also enjoyed his visits with Reverend Steigner, in part because he was Jake's friend, but also because the Reverend knew more about Sorrells than anyone else. Anytime Charlie tried to talk to Sorrells about the war, he changed the subject or turned a deaf ear, but the time had come when Eli believed he had a right to know.

Members of Reverend Steigner's congregation were often patients in Woodson's hospital, and he and his wife visited there almost daily. Eli stopped by to visit with Charlie one day before Helga arrived, and Charlie seized that moment to remind him of a remark he had made sometime earlier.

"Remember when you said Jake blew himself up?" Charlie asked early into their visit. "Why would he do that?"

Eli knew how much Charlie admired Sorrells, and that he had not asked an idle question. He paused for a moment, organizing his thoughts, choosing his words carefully. "You remember all I told you before?"

Charlie nodded and he went on. "All of that took place the first night, but Sorrells faced death almost constantly throughout the next four or five days. Two days before he was rescued, he banded with a small group of other Airborne survivors. They engaged hostile troops as best they could, and they eventually came upon the enemy protecting a bridge that allowed German troops to cross the Merderet River.

"Sorrells was a demolition expert. The pack he carried contained what he needed to disable the bridge and prevent the Germans from crossing, at least until repairs could be made. Time meant everything to the allies. The Airborne troops fought against vastly superior arms to give them that time. They couldn't destroy the enemy, but they could delay them.

The Germans had the high ground, and their machine guns defended the bridge, but the handful of Americans managed to disable them. Now the question was how Sorrells might set his charges under the bridge while it was swarming with German troops.

"He and another Airborne worked their way under the bridge and scaled one of the iron support columns to a position immediately under the bridge's surface. Their device would not be sufficient to bring down the bridge, but they hoped it would destroy enough of the surface to make it temporarily impassable.

"They could see the ongoing combat beneath them. At one point, a German tank overran the American position, and the few who survived the tank were bayoneted where they lay.

"Sorrells and the other man knew that all hope of their own survival was gone, but they resolved to complete their mission. His companion was killed by rifle fire as they were attempting to position the explosives. When Sorrells was unable to attach the explosive device, and thinking he was as good as dead anyway, he climbed the few remaining feet to the bridge surface. He hung onto the iron railings and held the explosive device until the last second before throwing it onto the bridge. By then, the Germans were within fifty feet of him. The bomb was ten feet from Sorrells when it exploded."

Charlie's eyes flew open wide. "But how ... how?" he stammered.

"I'm told that once in a great while, if you are very close to an explosion, the force of the blast pushes you away from the impact. In Sorrells' case, the blast threw him into the river. I've tried to tell him it was a miracle. God's will. He just laughs.

"The explosion put the bridge out of commission, and an Allied relief force arrived two days later. They were repairing the bridge when Sorrells was found washed up on the riverbank. The cold water had prevented him from bleeding to death, but he was deaf for weeks. He still doesn't hear all that well."

Charlie lay very still, almost as white as the sheet he pulled up to his chin. "He ... he's a hero," Charlie finally managed to say. "He could have died."

"Jake Sorrells believes he did die that day," Eli said softly. "Sometimes people get strange ideas and nothing can change the way they see things."

For some time, the two sat in silence, mulling over their private thoughts, and then Reverend Steigner continued. "Charlie, I'm going to suggest that you not mention this conversation to Jake. He may tell you, in time, but I doubt it. For my part, I believe God saved him for a purpose. If it was to keep Les Jones from killing you and Mrs. Marston, then you've been saved for a purpose too."

Before Reverend Steigner left the hospital that day, Charlie Conn knew the sort of man he wanted to grow up to be.

During Charlie's hospital stay, Sorrells and Eli had spent more time together than at any time since their days at the army hospital. During one of their visits, Eli turned the conversation toward Sorrells' postponed interest in John Marston.

"I think I should have something firm about Marston soon," he said. "Maybe as soon as tomorrow."

"That would be good," was Jake's terse but understated response.

"May I ask you what you intend to do? About Marston, I mean."

Sorrells fixed his friend with a steely stare. "Do you really want to know?"

"No, not normally, but I doubt if anything Marston has done would merit the kind of retribution you sometimes demand. Besides, should anything go wrong, there are Helga's feelings to consider."

"Eli, what the hell are you talking about?"

"I've been watching you two here at the hospital, and I think there's something building between you."

"That's another thing you may not want to know, Eli."

"Well, yes, but that's not what I mean." Mary and I believe there's some kind of feeling developing."

Sorrells' laugh had an empty sound to it. He didn't meet the Reverend's eyes when he said, "Eli, you know me better than that. I'm not the kind who forms attachments."

A smile crossed Eli's face. "Jake, my friend, you would be the last one to know. You wouldn't recognize human attachment if it bit you in the ass. Pardon me, but you know I'm right."

Sorrells shrugged and moved away, but Eli called after him, "And then there's the boy. You must know that he worships you."

Sorrells never looked back.

Chapter Twenty
Triumphal Entry

After two weeks of Helga's care and Charlie's access to Woodson's exceptional small-town medical facilities, it was hard to believe he had so recently been near death's door. Helga continued to read to him and fuss over him until the day came when the teenager rebelled against his confinement. The doctor agreed to his dismissal, and Charlie went home to convalesce at the ranch.

Helga viewed Charlie's homecoming as cause for celebration, and she spent much of the day before baking. A carnival atmosphere spread over the Marston Ranch, tempting Sorrells to steal unattended cookies almost as fast as they came out of the oven. Finally, enough was enough.

"Those are for Charlie!" she scolded the fleeing thief. As though he knew his best friend was coming home, even Pup perked up and joined in the fun.

Nothing could be salvaged from the bunkhouse fire. Sorrells cleared away most of the ruble, and he and Helga were considering how it could be rebuilt. The original structure was the product of John Marston's grand idea of how big the ranch might become. A considerably smaller building would be more appropriate, to their way of thinking. In the meantime, with Charlie home from the hospital, there would have to be a change in their sleeping arrangements.

Helga balked at the thought of transporting Charlie home in Sorrells' rough-riding pickup, and Sorrells agreed. He called Deputy Roy Strange, who volunteered to drop by and pick up Helga on his way to Woodson, and they would all ride back to the ranch together.

Helga had packed up clothes for Charlie to wear home from the hospital, including his new cowboy boots, which pleased him greatly. But then she helped him get dressed, and to add insult to injury, she scrubbed his face and combed his hair.

The hospital bill was no problem. The Mason boys had mailed Helga's packages to Clarissa's outlet as promised, and a sizeable check had been deposited to Helga's account, including an advance to cover half of the new order. Now it was up to Helga and the Dibs women to fill not only that order but others that continued to come in. It appeared that their enterprise would succeed.

Charlie was delighted to ride home in Deputy Strange's car, with its sirens, radio antenna and big shiny Sheriff's seal on the door. Helga gave up trying to get him to lie down in the back seat once he'd seen the official looking instruments and flashing lights on the dashboard, and she happily slipped into the back seat alone. She didn't care where Charlie sat as long as she was taking him home.

The trip back to the ranch required Deputy Strange to drive down Dibs's Main Street. When he slowed to conform to the thirty miles per hour speed limit, people on the street spotted Charlie sitting in front with the deputy, and they began to yell and wave. Charlie grinned and enthusiastically returned their waves through the open window. "It's almost like a parade," he yelled back at Helga.

Charlie Conn would never forget that minute or two of homecoming fame. Neither would Helga, who barely managed to choke back happy tears. In keeping with the occasion, Deputy Strange made an illegal U turn and drove back the direction they had come from, and more of the locals came out to the street to see what was going on. Others driving up Main Street pulled off to the side and got out of their cars to wave and cheer.

That night after supper, followed by an almost endless selection of Helga's finest sweets, the matter of temporary sleeping arrangements was settled without discussion. It was a given that Charlie would convalesce in the large bedroom at the front of the house; and, though Sorrells intended to bunk in the barn, Helga dismissed that plan. She insisted on making a pallet for him on the living room floor and he agreed to the arrangement.

As much as Charlie reveled in his homecoming, an excess of food combined with his weakened condition forced him to admit he was tired. Helga settled him in bed with a grateful and emotionally exhausted Pup nestled against him. Before she turned off the light, she bent down to kiss Charlie on the forehead. Without thinking, he found her hand and squeezed it. Words weren't required to express what they both knew in their hearts — that something greater than shared blood bound them.

Sorrells had slept on floors before, and he was sleeping soundly when, along about midnight, Helga pulled back the quilt that covered him and slid in beside him. Her arms reached out to pull him to her, and he didn't resist. In fact, he had been expecting her.

Charlie was about to discover the meaning of instant fame among the citizenry of one small Oklahoma town. He had been back at the ranch only two days before a steady parade of friends began to invade the ranch. They parked their pickups near the barn, examined the place where the bunkhouse had been, then walked solemnly through the barn to the stall where Sorrells had killed the villain, Les Jones.

"I say all three of them was heroes," was heard more than once, though Helga assured Charlie the two of them were heroes by association only.

The final stop was his bedroom, where Helga imprisoned the most famous teenage boy in Dibs. She was glad he had friends, and the cookie jar was always available to them; but Charlie was still convalescing, and she enforced strict visiting hours.

A good many of his visitors were kids who had chummed with him most of his life, but the circumstances of his home life and his eventual abandonment had made him different from them. All of that changed once Charlie Conn had a home where he was valued. Besides, he had been wounded in action. Real action.

Charlie proved to be more than equal to the role of local hero. He related every detail of the ambush to those who inquired, pulling up his T-shirt maybe half a dozen times a day to reveal his scars. "You think this is something, you ought to see Sorrells' chest," he sometimes said, much to Helga's displeasure. He was also capable of enhancing accounts of his own involvement in Jones' demise when necessity seemed to demand it, but never in her hearing.

At first, Charlie's visitors were all boys he had called friends, boys who had hung out together, either at school, when he attended, at the café or at the Saturday afternoon movies. But that was before a new dimension came bursting into his life, and her name was Jennie Lou Carson.

Like most small town boys, Charlie had never been schooled in social graces, besides which, he was naturally shy and awkward around girls. It was easier to pretend to prefer running around with boys rather than have a girl hanging on his arm.

Then one day Jennie Lou Carson came by for a visit. Her blonde, bobbed hair and freckled face had stolen his heart two years earlier when they were in junior high school, and now here she was, a gift from heaven as far as Charlie was concerned. He might have thanked God for letting Les Jones shoot him if that's what it took. Emboldened by his newfound fame, he affected an exaggerated limp as he carried lemonade from the kitchen to where they sat on the porch. He had no sooner settled into the swing beside her than he bolted out what was on his mind. "Jenny Lou," he said, "I was think'n that when I get up to it, we might see a movie some night soon ... real soon. I'm driving some, you know."

Jennie Lou smiled at him above the rim of her glass. "I'd like that," she said. "I'd like it a lot."

And so it began.

Chapter Twenty-One
Community Effort

Sorrells was eager to get started on rebuilding the bunkhouse, and Charlie was all in favor. Helga, too, realized the necessity, but Sorrells and Charlie were on their own with this one. She and the guild ladies had their hands full in the Dibs Library basement where the whir of a dozen sewing machines filled the air from dawn until dark. If she had any reservations, it was that she considered Charlie a member of the family, and she preferred to house him under her roof.

Finally, it was Charlie who won her over. "Mrs. Marston," he said, "I'm getting old enough to need a place I can think of as my own. I'd like to get back to live'n in the bunkhouse with Jake. It ain't that I don't like it here in the house and all, but me and Jake ... well, we're. ..."

With Charlie's help, the bunkhouse was approved, and Helga helped plan the new building. It was about time. Charlie was still slowed by his injuries, but he was a typical teenage boy, bored by inactivity and eager to get the new project underway.

Sorrells drew up a crude construction plan, and he helped Charlie with measurements. When they were satisfied, they took the plans to the lumberyard. "They'll have someone who can estimate what we'll need and what it will cost," Sorrells said. Money was no problem and wasn't likely to be in the future, judging by the number of boxes being transported from the library basement to the post office on the first leg of their journey to the California market.

The ranch, too, had begun to turn a profit, and the caliber of spring calves looked promising. Sorrells watched them cavort about their mothers in the pasture and was proud of his accomplishments. "Mine and Charlie's," he was quick to amend.

With the help of Fred Smith at the lumberyard, they were able to come in with a dollar figure that Sorrells felt would suit their budget. Fred volunteered to carry most of the expense during construction, which Sorrells figured would be complete about the time the calves were ready for market. When Sorrells told Fred that he and Charlie would come back in a couple of days to get the first load, he said, "You and that boy gonna be doing this yourselves?"

"We sure are," Charlie said before Sorrells could answer. "Me and Jake." There was such pride in Charlie's voice that Sorrells had to turn away.

But as much as he thought of the boy, his dedication to finding John Marston was never far from the front of his mind. Without making any commitments, Sorrells had felt out the Mason boys' willingness to hire on at the Marston Ranch in the spring and was encouraged by the response.

Sorrells would very likely be gone by then, though he questioned how Charlie would take to being abandoned again, this time by a man he had grown to trust. Helga was a survivor, but what did she know about what an almost sixteen-year-old boy needed? Would she be able to keep Charlie in line if he chose to rebel? That was the problem with … with building attachments. Sorrells would never allow himself to think the word love, let alone speak it.

The next morning soon after breakfast, Helga glanced out the kitchen window to see a cloud of dust rising in the west. She ran outside to investigate just as the first truck pulled onto the place.

Smiling faces filled the cab and neatly stacked lumber filled the bed of the truck, and of the next one and the next. Behind them, cars wended their way at a slower pace, their drivers choking on dust kicked up by the trucks.

Sorrells and Charlie rushed out of the barn where they had begun their chores and Helga ripped off her apron as she ran into the yard. Dibs citizens spilled out of the vehicles, not only men and women but teenaged boys. The women carried a variety of pots, pans, platters and sacks and headed for the house, and the men and teens began unloading the lumber.

"Where do you want this thing to go up?" asked a grinning Frank Smith when Sorrells got within hearing range. "We ain't got all day."

Sorrells was by nature a man of few words, but now he was speechless. Charlie, however, was not. "This way," he said, heading toward the site he and Jake had blocked off earlier in the week. "This here's the front and the toilet goes in the northeast corner. C'mon and I'll show you. Here, gimme one of those shovels," he ordered one of his friends. "With this many of us, it won't take long to dig the trough where the cement blocks go, and I wish you'd look! They're already layin' out the framing right there on the ground. Reckon they intend to put it together and raise it up whole onto the foundation once we've got it down. Pup, this here's no place for you right now. Best get up there on the porch where you won't be underfoot."

Halfway through the morning, the women laid planks across frames, spread them with cloths they'd brought from home, and laid out cups and urns of steaming coffee alongside platters stacked high with donuts. Helga was amazed to see it all disappear, though it never appeared that the worksite was short of even one worker. Equally amazing was the speed with which the new bunkhouse was rising up out of the ashes of the old, somewhat larger bunkhouse. The other one accommodated six bunks. This one would sleep four, but it would have the added convenience of a modest bathroom. Just a shower, a sink and a stool, but once the men got it hooked up to the windmill, it would be the finest in the area.

Lunch was several mountains of various sandwiches, gallons of sweet tea and dozens of pies laid out on the same planks and disappearing as magically as the donuts had, again while no workman's post seemed vacant. Thirty or more men and teenaged boys labored consistently throughout that day, and the finished bunkhouse stood on the spot where the old one had stood by the time the aroma of pit roasted beef filled the air. Streams of women passed back and forth between the kitchen and the plank table bearing all manner of vegetables, bread, every kind of dessert, and the ever popular sweet tea.

It was a tribute to this well-oiled machine that Sorrells, Helga and Charlie hadn't noticed the absence of those who had dug the pit out behind the house and tended the roasting between bouts on the ladder throughout that day. Pup had, and he was ecstatic.

After supper, while there was still enough light, the workers cleaned up, loaded up, and caravanned back to Dibs as quietly as they had come.

Helga stood at the window for a long time that evening, counting the blessings that had come to her when Jake Sorrells walked through her door. "This is what you wanted for me, isn't it, Mother?" she whispered. "I wish you could know how well things have turned out." The bedroom window curtain billowed on that still evening, but Helga was preoccupied and didn't notice.

Sorrells did, though. He stood in the bedroom doorway listening to Helga's whispered words, wishing she wouldn't attribute her happiness to a man who couldn't be trusted, who was already planning to leave, who would be gone by spring. When the curtain billowed, he turned soundlessly and left. He would spend the night with Charlie on the bunkhouse floor. They would drive into Woodson tomorrow and pick up what little furniture the bunkhouse needed at the army surplus store. Maybe they'd drop by and see Eli.

Chapter Twenty-Two
Oklahoma City Stockyards

The years' better than average rainfall had done a lot of good for the ranch's financial outlook. The grass was green and tall and the ponds were full. Sorrells had arranged for a local farmer to cut and bale the prairie grass hay, and with a little luck there would be another cutting in late summer. The bunkhouse had been rebuilt. The steers were ready to go to market. The price they brought would determine whether or not the ranch would show a sufficient profit to tide Helga over during the winter months when most income would stop. Except for her sewing projects, of course. That business seemed to be booming.

Charlie and Sorrells put in long hours every day, but Charlie had plenty of energy left to borrow the pickup for nightly visits to town. Sometimes Sorrells lingered in the house with Helga after Charlie had left. On those nights, the fervor of their lovemaking was undiminished, and the hours they spent alone together throughout the days were equally rewarding.

They often sat together, sometimes talking, sometimes not. She told him about the progress her new business was making but mostly about the friends that business had brought her. As a newcomer to the town, she'd had no friends except Melba. She knew that was because of the stories John had told about her, but things were different now... so very different. Most of all, though, she talked about Charlie, how proud she was of him, how much she hoped he would do well in school, how much having him there meant to her.

Sorrell's conversation was, for the most part, limited to the ranch, but Helga knew that important things would go unsaid. He erected a screen around him to keep others away, but there were other ways that he told her what she would never hear from his lips. His eyes could become fierce in anger, but they could also be soft, sometimes even showing wonder. She felt them on her when she was in the kitchen, or scattering grain for the chickens, or sometimes just walking across a room. Other times, when they were talking, or when she was reading a book, she would look up to see his eyes on her as if trying to somehow absorb her.

Sometimes he saddled the horses and they rode across the ranch to the hills that Sorrells had discovered the first week at the ranch. One evening, he lay beside the pond with his head in Helga's lap, her hand beneath his shirt running her fingers tenderly over the scars that marked his chest. He wrapped his hand over hers and sat up.

"I'm sorry," she said. Did I hurt you?"

"No. But I need to ask you something that might give you pain. You said your mother asked you to forgive her. What had she done?"

Helga would have pulled away had he not held her tightly. "I have already told you too much," she said. "Have you not guessed the rest?"

"No, and I wouldn't ask if I didn't need to know."

"Well then," she said after awhile, "I will tell you, but you must not judge my beautiful mother harshly."

"I don't have that right."

"No. No you don't. Neither do I." Helga sighed deeply and then she began: "John might have thought he was in love, but not with me. Not at the beginning. Not ever. I have told you that mother was desperate to get me out of Germany. To accomplish that purpose

— and for whatever safety a man in the house might assure the two of us living alone in lawless post-war Germany — she ... she agreed to become his lover.

"I overheard them arguing early in their relationship. She would not welcome him into her bed unless he agreed to claim me as his fiancée and arrange my passage to the states when his tour of duty ended. Mother was a beautiful and persuasive woman. Not long after, she handed me the necessary documents to be activated when transportation was available. I was one of the 20,000 war brides and fiancées to ship out of there in 1946. Others might say Mother's means to her desired end were extreme. No one who endured those war years would. She had lost her beloved husband and her son. She was determined that I should live.

"At any rate, John agreed to her conditions; he was sent back to the states six months later, and I set out for America with the first shipload of German war brides when my paperwork was finalized. I was 19 when we married. John was almost twice my age.

"I've told you how we happened to settle here in Oklahoma. I didn't tell you I had no sooner stepped inside the house than he was upon me, tearing at my clothing, ripping the pins from my hair. My screams were useless on these empty plains and they seemed to urge him on. I learned to endure in silence.

"John betrayed me and he betrayed my poor lonely, guilt-ridden mother. Throughout those first few weeks, before her suicide note arrived, I wrote to her daily, but never about how miserably her attempt to save me had failed. Not that it mattered. I found my unmailed letters in the box with his lady friend's letters after John left. I have no doubt he took perverse pleasure in leaving them where he knew I would find them."

They rode back to the house that evening in silence. Sorrells walked with her to the house. Before returning to the bunkhouse, he pulled her to him and held her tightly.

That night he lay awake in his bunk, staring up toward the dark ceiling. He had always done better when he had a single, driving purpose. Now he had one. Many possibilities ran through his mind. He'd had a letter from Eli Steigner telling him exactly where to find John Marston. The sooner the better, but first he had to sell the steers.

Helga, too, lay awake that night. Who was this Jake Sorrells that Reverend Steigner had brought to her? Such a strange man, his emotions pent up to the breaking point, then spilling over and lethal. There was a strength in Jake Sorrells that she hadn't anticipated. Not physical. That had been apparent from the moment she first saw him standing in her yard beside his spewing, decrepit pickup. His was a different kind of strength. Internal. She wondered at her willingness to share so much of her life with such a man.

At first light, Sorrells and Charlie began the long process of gathering the steers. The small sale barn in town didn't offer enough buyers to make it practical to sell Marston Ranch stock in Dibs. There were two stockyards that had enough buyers to maximize the price for the Marston stock. Most ranchers in the area shipped to the Oklahoma City facility. Sorrells talked it over with Helga, and it was agreed to send her steers there. He contacted the commission house and arranged for a truck to be sent to the ranch to pick up the Marston steers and overly mature cows.

It wasn't easy, but Sorrells convinced Helga that Charlie should make the trip with him. "This is an important part of the business," he said. "Charlie needs to meet the people we're dealing with at the stockyards."

As he and Sorrells continued to bring steers to the barn lot, it was evident that more than one truck would be necessary. The two of them would follow behind the hired trucks and be on hand at the stockyard the following day, then return to the ranch after the stock sold.

Charlie Conn had never seen anything so grand as the huge building that housed the commission, and the cattle pens at the yard appeared to go on for miles. The street was crowded with pickups and trucks waiting to unload the cattle they held.

After breakfast at the Cattlemen's Café the next morning, they walked to the yard to check on their stock. Buyers from local packing houses sat on high rail fences surrounding the pens that constituted the greater part of the bustling complex. When they were serious enough to talk price per pound, they left their perches to wander among the pens, touching as many of the steers as practical to determine weight and grade. Ranchers, whose profit for their year of labor and expense depended on a good price, waited anxiously for the buyers' decisions. Charlie and Sorrells waited with them.

All the sellers had sun and wind-tanned faces, and all were dressed the same. The boots and hats of some might be more expensive than others, but they were all cowboys and ranchers, and they valued their common heritage.

Helga's steers brought a good price and the mature cows a fair price. After adjusting for the cost of transportation and the commission house fee, the clerk handed Sorrells a check, which he handed to Charlie.

"This is Charlie Conn," he said. "Next year you'll be dealing with him." Later, in the pickup as they drove back toward Dibs, Charlie asked Sorrells what he had meant.

"Charlie, I'm a man that doesn't stay long at any one place," said Sorrells. "I figure that with the check we're taking back to Mrs. Marston, my job here is done."

Charlie stared straight ahead at the road for several miles before he trusted his voice. "I don't want you to go," he said. "I ain't talked to her about it, but I think Mrs. Marston wouldn't want you to go either."

"I appreciate that, Charlie. What you said means a lot. Most of the time when I finish a job, the people who hire me are more than pleased to see me leave."

"What kind'a jobs do you do for those people?" asked Charlie. Sorrells made no immediate response. Then slowly, measuring each word, he said, "Some people have problems they can't handle on their own. Problems that lawyers and even the law can't solve for them. I'm a man who can. I've seen justice done for people who can't get it any other way. I get paid for my skills, but I've never taken a job based only on the money. Hell, if money meant anything to me, I wouldn't have come to the ranch in the first place."

"What about me? What about Mrs. Marston? I know she'd want you to stay."

"You'll both be better off without me."

They drove northwest into dark, deepening clouds. Neither spoke again for many miles.

Chapter Twenty-Three
Tornado

The day before Sorrells and Charlie left for the Oklahoma City stockyards, they had stopped for gas in town. Billy Maples, one of the Marston Ranch hands Sorrells had fired, filled the tank. He and his sidekick, Joe Damron, had lounged about the Dibs pool hall until their money was gone and, when no one rushed to offer them employment, Damron left town.

The only work Maples could find in Dibs was at Milo Phillips' filling station, pumping gas, checking oil and washing windshields. Phillips knew what sort of help he had hired, but it wasn't easy to find a pump man who would work for forty-cents an hour.

No conversation passed between them as Maples filled their tank, but he overheard Charlie ask Sorrells about the cattle they were transporting that day. It wasn't until the following day that it came to him that he had almost missed a golden opportunity. The sale was going on now, and Sorrells and the kid wouldn't be back until late that night. He would have no reason to be afraid at the German woman's place that night.

He and Damron had been wrongfully fired. Maples knew where Sorrells had stored his valuables. He would go to the ranch and steal whatever he found that could be sold out of town, but he wouldn't make the mistake Les Jones had made when he moved in on Sorrells.

With luck, the German woman would be asleep. She wouldn't even know he was on the place.

While Maples plotted his theft, Helga paced the house in the muggy calm. The sky was still threatening, but the rain had stopped. Though the radio sputtered importantly, the words were all but unintelligible.

As the evening wore on, the clouds came and went, first threatening and then dissipating, but the humidity was a constant, leaving her skin clammy and uncomfortable. A bath helped. She stepped from the bathtub and, with a swipe of her hand, cleared the steamy mirror and examined her face. Hannah was right. The night cream was working.

She turned off the bathroom light, opened the bedroom window, and looked out into the yard. A section of gutter hung precariously from the roof, silhouetted against the flashing night sky. "Silly Pup," she scolded the dog beneath her bed. "Afraid of a rattling gutter."

She pulled back the spread and slid between the sheets, turning to watch the rolling clouds skid across the face of a white half moon. Where are those two? she thought. There's a storm coming, and they should have been home by now.

When Maples left work that night, he had his pay, a tank full of gas he had taken when old man Phillips went home for lunch, and an extra ten dollars he pilfered from the cash drawer. If all went as planned, it would be a long time before he would have to work another day for a lousy forty-cents an hour.

He was so sure of the plan he had devised that he whistled softly on his way to load up the contents of his rented room. Since he still owed his last two weeks' rent, he was careful to sneak his stuff out to the car without alerting Widow Bradley, who owned the boardinghouse and lived on the upper story. One more of Melba's good cheeseburgers and a couple of beers at the pool hall, and he was ready to make a profitable and, he hoped, an unobserved visit to the

German woman's place.

Helga was on the brink of sleep when an especially strong gust of wind threatened to dislodge the downspout. She closed the window against the rain that had begun in earnest, then found the switch on the bedside lamp and turned it. Nothing. The overhead light wasn't working either. Wind roared around the corners of the house and shook the window casements. That was it, she assured herself. The lines were down. Well, she and Pup didn't need the light right then anyway.

Two shorts and a long set her heart to pounding. She groped her way around the end of the bed on her way to the kitchen to reach the ringing phone.

"Hello?" she shouted above the wind.

"Helga, is that you?"

"Melba?"

"Get out of there! You're in danger. A couple of Maples' buddies say he's headed for your place, and not with good intentions. I got hold of Roy, and he's on. ..." The phone died in her hand.

It's looking good, thought Maples as he slipped and slid toward the Marston Ranch turn off. The sky had clouded over completely now, the wind was up, and a steady rain fell. It'll keep the woman in the house and cover any noise I might make, he thought. Wind blew leaves from the trees and set them to dancing in his headlights. He cut off the lights and eased the pickup through the muddy lane, then rolled to a stop next to the barn where Les Jones had spent his last moments on earth.

"Jones weren't noth'n but a damn drunken fool," Maples said aloud, proud of his own foresight in downing no more than a couple of beers at the pool hall. The sky was boiling as he slid out of his truck and ran into the barn.

Helga had never understood the weather in western Oklahoma. The very thought of a tornado was terrifying. She had seen the death

THE GERMAN WOMAN'S HIRED HAND

and destruction they left behind. She should have had a shelter dug, as many of her neighbors had.

As if it weren't bad enough that her own life was in peril of the storm, Charlie and Sorrells were out there driving through this, and now there was this Maples threat! "After our run in with Jones, you'd think we'd have had the foresight to stash a gun in the closet," she told Pup in exasperation.

Thunder roared without pause and bolts of lightning sliced the night sky. Helga mulled over Melba's warning and assured herself that, if he did intend to do her harm, she had survived the almost constant bombings in Berlin, and she could handle Billy Maples. Pup had begun to shiver even before the lights went out, and now she held him in her arms as she paced from window to window, listening to the loosened gutter crash against the side of the house outside her window and calculating the distance and ferocity of the oncoming storm. When she could wait no longer, she slid beneath the bed and scooted the shivering Pup in beside her.

Not far to the south, but further than they wanted to be, Charlie was turning the driving over to Sorrells. The old Ford was no longer able to do its fifty-miles an hour maximum and was hard put to creep along at thirty-five. Rain whipped sideways, the wind almost pushing the truck off the road. The vacuum windshield wipers were useless, but with Helga alone at home, there was no thought of stopping to allow the storm to pass by. They were only about twenty miles from the ranch, but the going was slow. Neither voiced his concern, but their hearts pounded, and they exhaled every breath through clenched teeth.

Maples turned off his flashlight to save his weak batteries and felt his way along the stalls that lined the center of the barn that he knew well, but now it seemed as though it would explode in the fierce wind. He would have to change his plan. The barn was not going to survive the storm. The house would be safer, but the storeroom was not a foot from where he was standing. First things first. He found a crowbar and ripped off the bracket securing the lock Sorrells had installed that first day at the ranch. Inside were five or six neatly arranged bundles wrapped in canvas. He opened one. The flickering flashlight revealed an assortment of weapons. How many guns were in that bag and how much money would they bring him? He would seek safety in the house from the storm and then return for them.

He selected a revolver, assured himself that it was loaded, and stuck it in his belt. Then he ran toward the house, dodging pieces of sheet metal ripped from the barn roof and tumbling along beside him. It would be a miracle if he reached the house in one piece. Even then, the structure might not be sturdy enough to withstand the storm, but anything was better than the creaking, wide-open barn.

A flash of lightning revealed the front door, and he flung himself toward it. Inside, all was dark. His flashlight in one hand and the pistol in the other, he stood stock-still, listening, while water dripped from his clothing onto the floor. The flashlight shook in his hand as he cast the beam about. There was no sign of the German woman. He was thinking the house might be deserted when he heard a dog bark.

He followed the flashlight beam to Helga's bedroom, straining to determine the layout as it pierced the darkness. Growling came from beneath the bed, and he figured he'd find the German woman there too. Maples had planned to steal what he could from the ranch and then slip away after the storm had passed, but now a madness swept over him. If he died in the storm, he wouldn't die alone.

"Damn you, bitch!" he swore, lowering the pistol to within inches of where Helga lay clutching the whimpering Pup to her chest. "I'll teach you to fire my ass!"

In that instant, his ears popped in the vacuum of the approaching tornado, and then it was upon them, a thousand freight trains roaring across the prairie night, magnifying a hundredfold the moaning of the house. Maples aimed the pistol, but before he could pull the trigger, the gutter came crashing through the window and a shower of glass shards exploded into the room.

The sound of tinkling glass had no sooner subsided than the earth stilled in the storm's aftermath, leaving behind an eerie calm. Helga rolled out from under the bed where Pup continued to cower. She had heard Maples declare he would kill her and had seen his shoes edging beneath the bed where she lay, and her choices of action had been limited. Should she remain where she was and wait to be murdered or try to flee the house? She had apparently made the right choice. As Helga had rolled out from under the bed, her fingers had encountered something wet and slippery. Now she moved her hand and touched the face of Billy Maples, who was lying on the floor beside the bed, his breath coming in jagged gasps.

The room was pitch black except for Maples' dimming flashlight on the floor where it had fallen. She snatched it up and trained its beam on his prone body, then knelt beside him and felt for a pulse. A shard of glass protruded from his neck, and his heart pumped his life's blood out onto the floor. She carefully worked the shard out of Maples' neck. Then, just as Sorrells had shown her to do for Charlie, she pushed down against the wound, but not so hard as to cut off his already limited air supply.

Her hands red with his blood, her knees slipping in the stuff, she remained there for what seemed like an eternity before she heard Charlie and Sorrells calling out her name, then the door banging against the wall and their muffled curses as they made their way to her through the dark house, bumping into furniture as they came.

"I'm here," she called out. And when their pace seemed too slow, "Help me! For God's sake, help me!" she screamed. Then Sorrells was touching her shoulder, surveying the situation in the diminishing beam of the flashlight that Charlie mutely held in one hand while he comforted the shaking Pup with the other. Sorrells pulled

Helga's hands away from Maples' neck and replaced them with his own.

"Charlie, you'll find candles and matches in the pantry," Helga said in a voice she didn't recognize. "The phone lines are down, too, but Melba called earlier. Roy should be here any minute."

As if on cue, the deputy's siren wore down outside the door and Roy was immediately on the radio summoning the town's new ambulance. It would be Billy Maple's dubious distinction to be the first to profit from the service the town board had voted in following Jones' attack on the Marston Ranch. The same town meeting where downtown streetlights and sidewalks were approved.

Once again, friends and neighbors rushed to the aid of the German woman's household, and Maples was soon on his way to the Woodson Hospital. Some of the neighbors had sustained damage to their own property, yet they had come without question in response to Roy's call for help. Even after they were assured that their neighbors were safe, they stayed on to mill about the Marston house nursing the inevitable cups of coffee, assuring themselves that all was right with their corner of the world and life as they knew it would go on.

The deputy stayed only long enough to hear Helga's account of what had transpired that night, and then, "I've got to see what damage has been done elsewhere," he said as he walked across the candlelit room. At the door, he turned to Sorrells and said only half in jest, "It don't hardly pay me to leave this place. I might as well have me an office out here."

It was past midnight before the neighbors returned to their own homes and Sorrells sent Charlie to find a tarp to cover the window whose one particular shard had almost certainly saved Helga's life. Sorrells stayed with her until long past dawn, his arm about her shoulders and holding tightly to her hand. Never had he experienced such a feeling of relief, nor of such pride, in how she had handled herself in all but impossible circumstances. Charlie and Pup remained curled up on the couch while Helga and Sorrells continued to sit side by side, touching, until dawn promised them a bright and cloudless new day.

Chapter Twenty-Four
The Mason Boys

As was often the case in the aftermath of a storm, McArthur's Mercantile and Fred Smith's lumberyard did a booming business throughout the next weeks, and the McCord's café profited from the spin off. The place was full to overflowing with locals who, since they were in town to pick up building supplies anyway, might as well stop by and sit awhile, catch up on the news, maybe take home a mess of Clem's barbecue to the family.

The guild ladies didn't miss a day at their sewing machines in the library basement, though the building did sustain roof damage before the tornado lifted and continued northeast, nipping at the Marston Ranch and neighboring spreads. No lives were lost, and there was standing room only in church that Sunday. People knew to thank God in the wake of a storm that might easily have taken many of them with it, as it had in the past.

Early in the week, Sid and Fred Mason loaded up their picks, shovels, and spades and headed for the Marston Ranch to dig a cellar to Helga's specifications. Pup helped when the digging got underway, but then a rabbit darted across the yard and he was gone.

To cope with the sandy terrain, the Mason boys lined the walls and ceiling with planks and supported the structure with verticals. When the cellar was pronounced finished, Helga would hang a shotgun from pegs worked into the wall and stash another shotgun at the top of her closet. Maples would likely go directly from the hospital to prison, but she would be prepared if another thief were so foolish as to come on her place.

One warm April day when the cellar was nearing completion, Helga took the boys a pitcher of lemonade and sat on the ground in the shade beside them as they mopped the sweat from their faces. "You'll be finishing up soon," she said, "and it looks like you've done me a good job."

Sid punched his brother on the shoulder and grinned. "Don't know about Frank, here, but I guess he's learning."

"That's what I wanted to talk to you about," said Helga. "You've both proven you're good with your hands, and you've stuck with this job when it wasn't easy. With me in town so much now that my fashion line has caught on and Charlie in school come fall, Mr. Sorrells is going to need some help. Would you be interested in hiring on here? You don't have to decide now, but I'd need to know. ...."

"No ma'am," Sid broke in. "There's no need to think on it at all. Frank and I were wondering what we'd do when this job was finished, and I was just joking about him. He learns real fast, and I guess I do too. Mr. Sorrells could probably teach us all we'd need to know, and Charlie, too. He's just a kid, but I've watched him work around here and he does a man-sized job."

Helga picked up the tray and stood. "Good, then," she said. "It's settled. We start at 7 a.m., so get a good night's sleep. I think you're going to like the work. I know I do, but it took awhile." She was gone with a wave and a smile while, behind her, the brothers were having trouble containing themselves.

The gun situation hadn't been so easy to settle. Sorrells balked a week or more before Helga managed to persuade him to teach her how to shoot. "Charlie, too," she insisted. "We never know when we might have to defend ourselves, and we might as well both be prepared."

Throughout the following days, the three of them set aside time to mount up and ride the short distance to the pond, where Sorrells set up targets against the bank. "To preserve the livestock," he said, "in case a shot goes astray." He didn't admit it right away, but Helga and Charlie both had a good eye, and he was pleased with their marksmanship. Maybe Charlie had an edge over Helga at first, but she was determined, and it paid off. Sorrells had to admit she was something to watch. She flexed her knees and spread her feet for balance, raised the butt of the shotgun to her shoulder, frowned in concentration as she aimed, then squeezed the trigger and braced for the recoil. More likely than not, her aim was true.

At other times, he watched her out of the corner of his eye and was astounded by the changes that had come over her throughout the past months. The sun had freckled her nose, and outdoor activity had put a sparkle in her eyes, but it was more than that. Helga was no longer the meek German war bride whose husband had beaten her into submission and then left her to fend for herself. She wasn't overly fond of castrating and dehorning, but she could brand a calf as fast and as efficiently as any of them, and she could repair all but the worst of the fence damage. The garden beside the porch was small, but she tended it well and her vegetables were a welcome addition to the table, as were the baked goods that came from her oven.

But more than that, Helga was a respected woman in the community, a businesswoman who was making a name for herself beyond the Marston Ranch, beyond Dibs, beyond the county, even far beyond the state. Sorrells would never understand a woman's desire to own such brightly colored, extravagantly embellished garments as the guild ladies were putting out by the truckload, but it was obvious that, at least in other parts of the country, there was such a desire. Someone had to be buying up Helga's merchandise. Her bank account was growing by leaps and bounds, and she paid her seamstresses well.

You wouldn't see her lavish jackets worn on the streets of Dibs, or her pillows on Dibs sofas, and not out at the Marston Ranch either, but it looked like change was afoot. Charlie's eyes were big when he brought Sorrells a handful of sketches he'd found in the trash, and Sorrells understood why. "Now that's more like it," he told Charlie. "A far cry from what she's been doing, but it makes sense to me."

"Yeah," said Charlie, "but the church might not like it. You don't see women in these parts wearing pants unless they're working in the field, and these sure don't look like nothin' you'd work in. Dig down in that stack and you'll find some that ... well, they're short."

Not long after Sorrells and Charlie made their discovery, the phone rang one evening after supper. Helga answered, but she didn't say much. Just stood there nodding her head, writing on a piece of paper for the longest time before she hung up and turned to face them.

"That was Clarissa," she said. "She likes my new designs, and...."

Melba had picked up on the two shorts and a long and had heard the good news as it was passed on to Helga. Hers was the first in a barrage of phone calls that went on far into the night as the news spread to every household by way of the party line. Before midnight, every soul in the area knew that Helga Heinke's House of Fashion was to be featured in *Fashion Today's* summer issue. Dibs, Oklahoma, was about to find its place on the map, and the town had Helga Marston and the nimble fingers of the guild ladies to thank for that.

They would be ready when the photographers and journalists arrived to interview the town folks and snap photos of the place where Helga Heinke's House of Fashion got its start. Women dug through drawers and resurrected items that she had created four or five years earlier and laundered them carefully, cherishing the tiny *hh* she embroidered in the corner of each item. Excitement ran high, and little by little, plans for an all out area-wide celebration unfolded.

In case Woodson's motel ran out of room to accommodate the

crowd they expected in addition to the Californians about to descend upon them, Widow Bradley would be ready for the overflow. A crew of teenaged girls armed with mops and dust cloths saw to that, and Amy down at McArthur's Mercantile dug through the back room and came up with matching slipcovers to disguise the worn parlor furniture.

Sorrells watched it all develop as he went about the ranch putting things in order, sharing with Charlie and the Mason boys his considerable farming and ranching knowledge. They picked it up eagerly, almost as if they weren't aware they were learning. Early evenings, Jake sometimes sat with Charlie on the banks of the pond, not talking, just skimming stones off the surface, watching Pup kick up his heels as all healthy, spirited dogs do, enjoying each others' company. But when the sun went down, Charlie opened his books in the bunkhouse and studied, and Sorrells took his place beside Helga in the bed that he would be leaving soon. Helga smiled through bright eyes and welcomed him beside her, but she was not deceived. She had read the signs. Their time together was running out.

Chapter Twenty-Five
Finding Marston

It was becoming difficult for Sorrells to leave the ranch without Charlie wanting to go along, as though he feared that each trip would be the one from which Sorrells had told him he wouldn't return. He checked his cash reserve and knew he had enough to cover what he planned. Then, while Charlie and the Mason boys were out checking the stock, he pulled onto the road and headed west.

Ned Osment's garage was located at the edge of town on what had once been a small farm. The garage was a simple barn-like building near the road. The house he and his wife and kids lived in was further back, ringed by scrub timber. Between the house and Ned's shop, a dozen or so cars sat in various stages of disrepair. Ned called them parts. His wife called them eyesores.

He pulled his pickup into the yard and shut it down in front of the manual gas pump that Ned kept for his own use. Ned pulled his head out from under the hood of his current project and wiped his hands with a red shop rag as he went out to greet Sorrells.

"How you doing, Mr. Sorrells? How's Charlie getting along?"

"Charlie's just fine, thanks. He's coming along. I might be interested in buying some sort of car. You got anything?"

Ned's face broke out in a wide grin. "Well sir, if I don't, it ain't gonna take me too long to come up with something. You got anything special in mind?"

"I need something I can depend on. I don't much care what it looks like."

"Well, sir, lets us take a walk back towards the house. I got something back there I was sort'a think'n I'd fix up for myself. If it was to suit you, we'll see what we can work out. My wife's been on me to move some of this stuff. She don't think havin' these cars near the house is very pretty."

The car Ned showed Sorrells was a 1946 Ford business coupe. Unlike the rest of the cars in Ned's collection, this one looked like it was drivable. When he asked, Ned said it was. "This here is the car that the county confiscated from them bootleggers awhile back. I bought it at the auction."

"How's the engine?"

"That's why I bought it. Them bootleggers make sure they got good equipment. This here car will run like a scalded cat. If I keep it, I'll make a race car out'a it. Course I'd check it out for you before you put down any kind of cash."

"It's pretty much what I had in mind," Sorrells said. "How much?"

"You gonna want to trade in your pickup?"

"No, I've got something else in mind for you to do to the pickup."

After he and Ned had settled on the Ford coupe and what he wanted done to the pickup, Sorrells asked him to keep the transaction to himself. "Get the Ford ready to go. I'll bring the pickup in and leave it with you," Sorrells added.

When he got back to the ranch, Charlie, disappointed that Sorrells had left without him, asked Sorrells where he had been. "Had a little business in town," Sorrells replied.

The bunkhouse had been rebuilt and the storm damage repaired. Helga had her cellar, and the Mason boys were working out even better than he'd thought they would. The steers had been sold, the hay baled, and Helga's operating money was coming in hand over fist.

Sorrells clicked off the list in his mind. With Helga's help, Charlie could handle the usual teenage problems, and the younger Mason boy, Fred, was working into a friend. Fred was okay. Several years older than Charlie, but they'd attended a couple of movies together, and they seemed to enjoy each other's company.

Jake's personal list was shorter — find John Marston and deal with him. The list he had made in Helga's behalf might be complete, but his was not. Being careful not to wake Helga, he rose before dawn the next morning and left the house, but instead of checking the cattle, he crept into the bunkhouse and removed his duffel from under the bed. Pup thumped his tail on the plank floor and Charlie turned over, but they were both still asleep when Jake silently left the bunkhouse. He threw the duffel into the cab of his truck, then went into the barn and carried out the bundles he'd had with him when he came to the ranch, less the two shotguns he was leaving with Helga. They would be all that was left to show he had ever been there. Before he climbed into the pickup, he turned to look back toward the house. No matter what he was taking away, he was leaving something very valuable behind. He lit a cigarette, climbed into the cab, turned the truck around and headed toward Dibs.

Dawn was just breaking when he got to Ned's garage, routed him out of bed and picked up the keys to the Ford. Ned had been better than his word. The Ford was shiny even in the dim light. Jake transferred all his possessions to the Ford, thankful that the business coupe had no rear seat.

"Take the pickup out to the ranch when you're finished," he reminded Ned. "They'll need it."

"You got it," Ned replied.

Sorrells slid behind the wheel of the Ford and pushed the starter. The engine roared to life, and he smiled for the first time that day.

The café was opening when he drove through town. He considered stopping for a cup of coffee, but he didn't want to see anybody he knew very well just then. The Ford surged down the road toward Lawton and Ft. Sill.

He had been gone about three hours when Charlie woke. Out of habit, he looked over at Sorrells' bunk. It was made up army style, but it always was. Sid and Fred hadn't arrived yet, so he knew he wasn't late for breakfast. He dressed hurriedly and whistled Pup out from under his bunk. Maybe Jake was already at the house, but something seemed wrong. He checked the small bathroom. His shaving equipment was missing. On his way out the door, he checked under Sorrells' bunk. His duffel bag was gone. His pickup wasn't parked beside the barn. Maybe he had gone into town, but why take all his stuff? There was one more place to check. The storage room in the barn was empty too. Charlie ran to the house, choking on the words he would have to tell Mrs. Marston.

Helga was buttering the breakfast toast when Charlie brought her the news. She set a glass of milk in front of him, then carried her coffee cup to the table. Before she took her place, she patted Charlie's shoulder. "I know how much he means to you. I'm sorry," she said softly.

Charlie reached up to touch Helga's hand. "Both of us, ma'am. He means a lot to both of us."

Helga's heart sank, but the emotion never reached her face. She was surprised to hear her voice come out airy and cheerful when she said, "That's true, Charlie, but we have each other, and we'll learn to go on without him. He came here to help me in difficult times. Now he must believe he has done his job, and so he has gone. We'll miss him, certainly, but he has his own life to live, a life that doesn't include us. Remember this. It was Jake Sorrells who brought you to me. For that I will always be grateful."

The Mason boys' arrival cut their conversation short, which was good for both of them. Charlie had been as near tears as he'd ever been, and tears wouldn't do in the presence of the older boys. He finished his milk, grabbed up a piece of toast and rushed out to join Sid and Frank in the day's pursuits.

Helga sat alone at the table trying to adjust to an idea of the life she and Charlie would lead at the ranch without Jake. She wanted to cry, too, but tears had never served her well. Finally, she slapped the palms of both hands on the tabletop and stood up. "It's not impossible," she told the empty kitchen. "Charlie and I will make it work." It was work she needed. Hard work. The journalists and photographers would be there day after tomorrow to promote her fashion designs, and she had lists of things to do before she was ready for them.

She finished up the kitchen and was heading for a bath when reality hit her. She flopped back down in her chair to think. Her list of chores required considerable running around, and she had counted on Sorrell's pickup to get her where she needed to be. Well, her transportation was gone now. Gone with the man who had kept her world turning for almost a year. She grabbed up a tea towel to wipe away the rush of tears that fell of their own accord. "Damn him," she said. "Damn him for making me. …" The word "love" might have come to mind, but she wouldn't allow herself to speak it. "For making me depend on him," she finished.

She was as in control of her emotions as she would be for some time when she stepped from her steamy bath with what she thought was a workable plan. Melba answered the phone as though she'd been waiting for it to ring.

"Melba," she said, " Sorrells is gone and I need to get to Woodson to buy a car and pick up some things for Thursday's blowout. Do you think you could take me?"

"Sure," she said, "if it can wait till the noon rush is over. When will Sorrells be back?"

"Maybe never," said Helga, "but now's not the time to talk about that. I'll see you when you get here."

Melba was still talking when Helga hung up. They had both heard the party line receivers click. Helga would tell her what she needed to know when the time came, and they would decide how much to share with the community.

Chapter Twenty-Six
Parade Preparations

Melba left the cleaning up to Clem and the boy they had hired to help out at the café during spring break, and was pulling to a stop in front of Helga's house a good hour before she expected her. Helga left the boys' supper simmering on the back of the stove and grabbed up her purse. They were on their way in a matter of minutes.

A spontaneous "Wow!" escaped Melba's lips as Helga stepped off the porch and hurried toward the car, the lightweight wool of the slacks she wore swirling about her ankles. Must be that new color they're calling mauve, she thought, wishing for a fleeting second that she herself were less involved with the bookkeeping side of their business and more involved with the fashion side. Maybe she would ask Helga to make a pair of those for her. Goodness knows there were a jillion pairs of slacks packed up and ready to ship out, but nothing close to the size Melba would need. Some of the church folks might not approve of women wearing pants, but the guild ladies hadn't balked at turning them out as fast as they could to fill the orders that lined their pockets with more money than any of them could have imagined.

The town fathers weren't objecting, either. Money was flowing, and Dibs had streetlights, sidewalks and, the pride of the community, a shiny new ambulance to pay for. They had been more than willing to turn the library basement over to Helga's House of Fashion crew, and she had been more than willing to pay the utilities. There was no telling how much money the upcoming celebration would profit the community, what with the entire county expected to show up.

Roy would lead Thursday's parade in his official deputy car with the shiny Sheriff's seal on the door and the siren blaring, but the new ambulance would be the star of the day. The football team had drawn lots for the privilege of balancing on the fire truck's running boards, clinging to whatever finger-holds they could find.

"Where to?" said Melba as Helga slipped in beside her. She studied her friend's face for signs of stress and found them. Her eyes were puffy but her smile was brave. Melba wisely left it at that.

"I need a car," Helga said. "Any ideas? Something brand new and durable. Dependable. Low upkeep. Not a guzzler. Something that will be around long enough to grow old with me."

Melba might have asked if she was talking about a car or a man, but she left her thoughts unspoken. "How about a Cadillac?" she said with a grin. "A red one like Clarissa's if we can find it. Something you can drive off the lot with a warranty. Four doors would be best, and a big trunk for hauling stuff. Oh, and a radio. We'll walk around the lot and kick tires like we know what we're doing."

Helga gave her the smile that Melba had been working for. "I think we need an expert in on this deal," said Helga, "so I phoned Betsy. Jim will be waiting for us at Sam Johnson's Car Lot on the west side of Woodson."

Melba nodded her approval of the plan and, to fill the silence said, "You're looking good in that outfit, Helga. Good color. Good fit. And I like what Hannah's been doing with your hair."

Helga smiled her thanks. They would get around to discussing what mattered later. For now, she was grateful for her friend's diplomacy. "Thanks," she said. "Short hair is sure a lot easier to take care of, and slacks are a lot more comfortable than a skirt. More modest, too, if you think about it. They did make quite a stir when I wore them to the grocery store last week, but only one mother objected to letting her daughter model them for the photographers."

"Really. I didn't think there'd been so much as a ripple. Who objected?"

"Francis. Jennie Lou's mom. You know, Robert Carson's wife? She doesn't get out much, and I think I know why. She's the only guild member who doesn't sew with us, but I'll bet she'd like to if Robert would give her a little leeway. I think he must keep her on a short leash. You know. Like it was with John and me before he left."

Melba nodded and, after awhile, Helga went on. "Anyway, her husband is an elder in the church. He quoted her something in the Bible. Deuteronomy, I think it was, where it says a woman in men's clothing is an abomination to God."

"Helga, honey, a man would have to be blind to say you don't look like a woman in that outfit," said Melba. "I wish I could fit into something like it."

"Oh, but Melba, you could. I had no idea you were interested. I've got just the right fabric at the house, and slacks don't take more than an hour or so to whip out. It's nothing like all that piecing and quilting we do on our patchwork line, to say nothing of the time it takes to sew on all that trim. Sometimes I dream about those millions of sequins, feathers, and rhinestones, and I'll bet the others do too. Come on out to the house tonight and I'll whip up a pair for you while you help Charlie with his math. If you like them, you can model them tomorrow at the high school auditorium."

Melba's laugh started low and progressed to a guffaw. "Roy Strange would drop dead in his tracks if he saw that, and there's no telling what Dad would say. How about I model in Jennie Lou's place? You might start a fashion line for larger women. Goodness knows there are enough of us big beautiful girls who have been waiting a lifetime for a chance to strut our stuff." Melba was laughing so hard that she considered pulling off to the side of the road, but not Helga.

"I'm serious," she said. "We'll call the line Big Is Beautiful, and you have the face and body to prove it." Melba was speechless, but Helga went on. "Oh," she said, "I guess I didn't finish my story. Francis and Robert got their deal worked out, and Jennie Lou will be modeling after all. I called Reverend Steigner to ask him about Robert's scripture, and he and the Carsons had a talk. He told them if pants were good enough for Rosie the Riveter, they were good enough for women in this part of the country who work in skirts alongside their husbands no matter how deep the snow. He said he figured it was only right for them to be warm too. I thought that last part might be overkill, since the slacks I make aren't designed for field work, but it worked. Jennie will be modeling tomorrow. And, Melba, so will you."

"What?" This time Melba did pull off to the side of the road. They had entered Woodson and she needed a root beer. They could get one at the new Dairy Queen.

"I know you weren't serious when you mentioned it, and you didn't think I was serious when I agreed, but the idea of a line of clothes for larger sized women struck a chord with me. I believe we're onto something. We'll spring it on the photographers when they get here. In fact we'll feature you. Won't Clarissa be surprised! We'll get Hannah to style your hair. She's already agreed to do the models' makeup, and. ... Oh, Melba, if we could get Robert to let Francis breathe a little, wouldn't that be grand?"

Helga's smile faded. When the time came for her to say what she needed to say, it wouldn't be about her fashion line. Damn Robert Carson for lording it over his wife; damn John Marston for the hideous things he had done to her for so long. And damn Jake Sorrells for not knowing he loved her.

"Two root beers," Melba told the girl at her window.

"Make those root beer floats," said Helga. "It's on me. The car I'm going to drive home today is long overdue. If we aren't celebrating anything else, we'll celebrate that."

Chapter Twenty-Seven
Baby Blue Chrysler

Jim was poking around under the hood of a flashy black and yellow 1932 Ford Roadster when Melba and Helga pulled into Sam's Car Lot. Sam's son Bert had modified it, and there was no mistaking the pride in his voice. "You should'a seen it when Bert got hold of it," he said. "Nothing but a frame and a bunch of pieces handed down from my dad."

"A lot'a power and not much weight," said Jim, a recognized authority on hotrods. "What'll it do?"

"California's running them upwards of a hundred and forty," said Sam, "but Bert won't be doing more than half that."

Jim grinned. "You better watch him close. Looks like the kid knows what he's doin'. Chopped top, channeled body, pinched frame, dropped axles. All it needs is a set of them wide tires the serious racers are usin' out west."

"What's this?" asked Melba, waving her root beer straw at the object of their discussion. "If it's the sort of thing you have in mind for Helga, you're way off base."

"Oh, hi, Melba, Mrs. Marston," said Jim. "I didn't hear you drive in. No, this here ain't the right car for you, Mrs. Marston, but Charlie sure would appreciate it. What's Jake up to? You got him tied down at the ranch? I'da thought wild horses couldn't keep him from bein' in on the kind'a deal Betsy says you got in mind. Buyin' a new car ain't nothin' a woman ought'a do alone in a hurry."

Helga glanced down at the mention of Jake's name, and then flashed him a smile. "That's what we have you here for," she said brightly. "What do you and Mr. Johnson have in mind for me?"

Melba shook her head when she caught Jim's eye and lightened the exchange with, "Nothing painted black and yellow, I hope."

Sam motioned the ladies toward the showroom, where Jim had already checked out a pale blue Chrysler and pronounced it perfect. Now he stepped back while Sam showed Helga a couple of other cars on the floor, slamming doors, pointing out the qualities of each until he came to the car Jim preferred, and then he didn't say a word. The Chrysler was the sort of car that could sell itself, and it did.

"This calls for a real celebration," said Melba after the paperwork had been completed, Jim had been thanked, and Sam had handed Helga the keys. "I'll need to check in at the café, but if it looks like Dad and the boy can handle things there, I've got a bottle of wine that has celebration written all over it. What do you say?"

Charlie and Pup greeted Helga with enthusiasm when she drove into the yard. It was good to see Charlie smiling. She hadn't been sure what shape he'd be in after he'd fully digested the probability that Sorrells wasn't coming back. She tossed him the car keys. "Take it for a spin if you'd like," she said, "but no Pup allowed. Not with those muddy feet. Don't be long, though. Melba's coming out later to help you with your math. Come on, Pup. Let's get supper on the table."

That evening while Charlie was trying to concentrate on the math assignment that he and Melba would go over, Helga looked up from the slacks she was cutting out on the dining room table and said as evenly as possible, "Charlie, when Sid and Fred get here in the morning, I wish you'd tell them I want to talk with them. We need hands who are willing to bunk here on the ranch now that. ...

Well, we just do, and I hope one or both of them will be willing. You'll tell them for me, won't you, Charlie?"

Charlie stared at the lined notepaper he had been figuring on and nodded. "He's not coming back," he finally said.

"No, Charlie, I guess not." The clock tolled the hour before she continued. "It hurts, Charlie. I know it does. It hurts me too. But we've still got each other ... and Pup. We'll be okay. As long as we're together, we're going to be fine. Well, not fine. At least not right away." Helga laid her hand along the back of his neck, and he looked up to see tears in her eyes. "Oh, Charlie," she said when she could, "just promise me you'll stay. That you'll always be my family, even after you graduate and maybe go on to college if you want to. Just promise me that, will you, Charlie? And I promise never to do this to you again. To be such a bawl baby, I mean. Not to ... to smother you no matter how much I want to. Okay?"

When he didn't answer, she looked down at the pencil moving across his notepaper and broke one of the promises she had just made. Over and over, line after line, she saw through her tears that he had spelled out the word "Mom."

"Would it be okay?" he asked. "Would you care if I called you mom?"

"No, I wouldn't care," she said, hugging his shoulders. "I can't tell you how proud I would be ... how proud I am to be the mother of Charlie Conn. Now give me a hug. Melba just drove up and I've got to get these slacks in there to the sewing machine."

Chapter Twenty-Eight
Last Minute Plans

Sorrells had arrived in Lawton shortly after noon on that day and spent almost an hour driving around to get a feel of the city. Then he parked the Ford on Main Street and walked the downtown area until he found what he was looking for. "Lawton Chamber of Commerce" read the big black letters stenciled across the storefront window. He thought for a few minutes, working out what he would need to say before he pushed the door open and stepped inside. A middle age woman rose from her desk and stood to greet him.

He affected what he hoped was a benign smile, shook her extended hand and gave her the first name that came to his mind. "My church is trying to make calls on new families in town," he said, "a sort'a welcoming gesture. If the Chamber has a list of new arrivals, it would sure make our job a lot easier."

"I'm sorry," she said, "but we don't. Have you tried the utility companies? I'm sure they have that kind of information. What is your church?"

"Bible Baptist," he said, grabbing a name out of the air. "We're a small church, just getting started."

"I love small churches," she replied with a smile that gave Sorrells a twinge of guilt. "They're so friendly. I'm a Baptist myself. You know, I've got a friend at the electric company. Let me call her and see if she will give us a list."

"Bless you," he said, inwardly cringing at the sanctimonious smile he was sure his lips had assumed.

He picked up the list at the electric company, thanked the lady who had typed it, and folded it into the envelope she provided. "Bless you," he said again, flashing the same smile he'd left with the chamber of commerce lady. It occurred to him on the way out that he was getting good at deceiving helpful female public servants, and he wasn't all that proud of the talent.

He walked to the Ford, opened the envelope, and came across John Marston's name halfway down a list of some forty or fifty relatively new subscribers. His address and hook-up date were there, too. As an afterthought, Sorrells returned to the chamber office, thanked his new friend for her help and asked her if the chamber of commerce had a map of the city. They did.

It was late in the afternoon and he hadn't eaten, so he pulled the Ford into a drive-in, ordered a hamburger and a cup of coffee, and unfolded the map. Finding the general location was no problem. The rest was just a matter of driving the street till he found the mailbox bearing the number he was looking for. It was a typical army town house, red brick veneer and frame construction, single-car garage. The surrounding houses were of similar design and construction. The garage door was closed, and Sorrells' saw nothing that would indicate that anyone was inside. A few cars were parked at intervals along the curb. Sorrells pulled in behind a Nash half a block down the street. It was nearly six o-clock. People would soon be coming home from work.

He knew from experience to approach the house after dark or in the early morning hours. When he confronted John Marston, he would try to do it elsewhere. Or maybe not. There were many places to confront him. Shortly after six o'clock, a late model Lincoln sedan pulled into the driveway of the house Sorrells was watching. He started the Ford and drove by slowly. Marston wore a suit and carried something that could have been some kind of sample case. He unlocked the front door with a key from a ring of keys that he pulled from his suit pocket and entered the house.

Marston hadn't pulled the Lincoln into the garage. Perhaps he would be using it again tonight. One thing was certain, a strange car either parked or constantly driving down a residential street like this one would be viewed suspiciously by neighbors. He would need to move against Marston as soon as possible. His hand dropped to the starter button when Marston came out of the house and walked to his car. He was wearing slacks and a loud Hawaiian print shirt. Sorrells watched as he backed out of the driveway and started down the street. Then he fell in behind him, keeping about half a block distance between them.

He trailed the Lincoln to just outside the city limits where a row of beer joints might as well have had "Welcome G.I.s" spelled out in neon above the doors. Marston pulled his car into a long, graveled parking lot shared by three of the beer joints. Sorrells parked ten yards away and watched as he walked into a dive called "Horny Toad." He waited ten minutes. Then, his heart pounding in anticipation, he pushed the door open and walked in. Even in the dim light, Marston was easy to spot through the clouds of smoke. His loud shirt stood out in sharp contrast against the rest of the patrons, whose fatigues ran to olive drab. He was sitting at a dark corner table with an attractive woman a fraction his age.

Sorrells settled in at the bar among several young men whose hair was cut to their scalps. When the bartender asked what he would have, he said, "Coffee."

The bartender smirked. "You ain't drinking?" he said.

"Working," Sorrells replied. "I don't drink when I'm on the job."

"Me neither," the bartender mumbled.

"Who's the guy at the corner table with the shirt?" Sorrells asked, nodding his head in that direction.

"He's a jerk. Comes in here all the time, always throwing his weight around. One of these days somebody's going to mop the floor with him," he sneered. "What's he to you?"

"He looks like somebody I used to know. Who's the girl he's with? She looks a little young for a guy like him."

"That's something else he does that pisses me off. The girl's got a husband over in Korea, and here she is, screw'n that clown."

"Thanks," Sorrells said as he slapped down a dollar bill and slid off the barstool.

Outside, he breathed in deeply to clear the smell of beer from his nostrils as he walked to his car, where he sat waiting. A few minutes later, Marston and his girlfriend came out of the bar, got into the Lincoln and drove back to his house.

Sorrells drove around till he found a seedy tourist court and checked in under an assumed name. He pulled the Ford as close to the cabin door as possible and locked it. Once inside his room, he left the door open and raised the window in hopes of removing the stale air, and then he lay down on the bed and tried to sleep.

Melba didn't leave the Marston Ranch that night until the wine bottle was empty and Helga had opened another one. While she tailored Melba's slacks, she spoke of Jake Sorrells, but without tears. She admitted surprise at feeling so great a loss at his leaving, but Melba wasn't surprised at all. She knew Helga had been in love with Jake almost from the beginning, but she would let her figure that out on her own.

The clatter of the sewing machine filled the room while their thoughts pursued separate courses, and then Helga said, "What about Charlie? Am I going to be able to meet his needs throughout his teen years? I don't mean money. It looks like we'll be okay on that score, but Charlie's birthday is coming up. The first thing every sixteen year old wants is a drivers license, and after that they're gone."

"Charlie's a good boy," said Melba. "He's going to get into trouble like all kids do, but I doubt it's going to be serious. Besides, all of Dibs has a stake in that boy. They're not going to let him get too far out of line."

Helga whipped the slacks off the ironing board and held them up for Melba to see. "Here," she said. "Put these on so I can mark the hem."

"And another thing," Helga said as Melba slipped one foot and then the other into the slacks, "Sorrells taught him to drive, and he taught him well, but then he drove off in the pickup Charlie loved. I guess I could get him another one, but. ..."

"But you've already bought one car," Melba finished for her, "and back to back purchases that big. ... Well, it just doesn't make sense."

Their conversation bounced from one subject to another, all of it related to Jake, Charlie and Roy in one way or another while Helga completed the outfit that they both pronounced perfect.

"My butt never looked so good," Melba said, turning this way and that in front of Helga's floor-length, three-panel mirror. "Do I ever have a surprise for Roy! We've been talking about getting married, and these might just tip him over the edge."

"Don't forget to set your alarm clock," said Helga as Melba was leaving with the first of what would be many Big Is Beautiful ensembles draped over her arm. "Hannah is working you in before her 8 o'clock appointment," Helga called after her. "She said she's got a tight schedule, so it's then or never."

The camera crew started rolling into Dibs the next morning, all but eclipsing the next day's parade. The bottom floor of Widow Bradley's Boarding House filled up fast. She rented out her upstairs living quarters, packed up her three cats and moved in with her sister for the duration.

Dibs ranchers, those who had room, boarded horses that area rodeo clubs would ride in the next day's parade, and some of their owners bedded down in the barns beside them. Melba hired a string of high school students to help at the café. She would double that number the next day when carloads of people from neighboring towns would drive in for the Helga's House of Fashion festivities bringing their kids and their cash, and Dibs would be ready for them.

Helga spent most of the day before the event with a portion of the guild ladies in the library basement sprucing up their workshop, making it picture perfect for the photographers. Most of the other guild ladies were at home preparing food to be sold at concession stands. Others oversaw crews making banners while their husbands were at the high school auditorium constructing a runway that jutted out from the stage almost twenty feet beyond the first four rows of seats.

Chapter Twenty-Nine
Marston's Convinced

On the morning of Helga's big day, Sorrells had risen early and driven to a Lawton café for a quick breakfast. By eight o'clock, he was parked on Marston's street, where he discovered they did not share the same hours. A little after nine, Marston came out in his pajamas to get his paper. An hour later, he left for the day. Sorrells hoped that was a daily routine. If it was, he had his plan.

Sorrells presented his military identification card to the guard at Fort Sill's main gate and asked directions to the PX. Ten minutes later, he had purchased a package of professional looking paper, a box of envelopes, a cheap fountain pen and a bottle of black ink.

Throughout the next few hours, Sorrells walked the sidewalks of historic Fort Sill, enjoying the sights and sounds of the U.S. Army, both past and present. A young private directed him to the burial site of the great Apache Chief, Geronimo. As he stood near the grave, he could all but hear his fellow Screaming Eagles shout the chief's name as they pushed through the jump doors and hurtled into space.

That evening, mainly because he didn't want to spend more time than necessary in the musty tourist court cabin, he followed Marston on his nightly visit to the area beer joints. Sorrells could probably have taken him anytime he chose, but if he hurried it, he couldn't accomplish all he had set out to do. For that, he would need the help of two witnesses.

Helga woke on the day of the Dibs area-wide celebration to find herself alone in bed for the third consecutive morning in what seemed like a lifetime. She ran her hand over Sorrells' side of the bed and a surge of loss washed over her, no less painful than it had been the morning he disappeared into the pre-dawn dark. She had known that time would come, had felt it looming, helpless to stop the tide. What was it about her that caused a man to leave her like that? Not that she hadn't welcomed John Marston's departure, even prayed for it, but Jake was. ... Well, with him it was different. Comfortable. No, not just comfortable. There was something more. Helga threw her legs over the side of the bed and stood up. "A good deal more," she told the rooster crowing outside her window, but it wouldn't do to lie there feeling sorry for herself. This day promised to be the biggest day in Dibs' history, and she had better get up and help make it happen.

The journalists and camera crew were scheduled to arrive at the ranch by ten. She would follow them back to the library basement after lunch, where they would interview the guild ladies and take more photos. Deputy Strange had announced that the parade would commence at two o'clock sharp, followed by the much-touted style show at the high school auditorium. The Adams family had put together a banjo and fiddle group, and they'd brought in a harmonica player from Woodson. The town crew had worked all night installing two of the four streetlights waiting to be erected. There would be a street dance later on in the evening, but without Helga. The

Carsons had agreed to let Jennie Lou attend the dance with Charlie, so he would be needing the car.

The magazine publicity crew arrived at the Marston Ranch on schedule, a good deal of coffee was drunk all around, Helga had answered the journalist's questions and posed where the photographer told her to stand or sit. His flashbulbs clicked nonstop all the while. He captured several shots of her at Melba's old sewing machine, one of which would appear in glossy color on the cover of *Fashion Today's* summer issue. The publicity would send her clothing line zooming. Dozens of photos were taken of the ranch in general, but none of Charlie and Pup, who were nowhere to be found. Smart boy, Helga thought. They could be in the cellar, or they might have run off to town with the Mason boys until time to do evening chores. More than likely, though, Charlie was out at the pond skipping stones off the water, throwing sticks for Pup to retrieve, working out problems of his own. Helga wished she were with him.

Roy and his deputy's car had taken their official place as Grand Marshal at the head of the line when Clarissa Fontaine, a.k.a. Sadie Dale, screeched her big red Cadillac to a stop in line behind him. Wild horses couldn't have kept her from making an appearance at the biggest celebration her hometown had ever known. None of it would have been possible without Melba McCord, her friend Helga Heinke Marston and herself, the young girl who had run away in disgrace and made good. Sadie Dale had come full circle.

And so it was that the shiny white ambulance, pride and joy of Dibs, relinquished its place and pulled out behind the red Cadillac in that day's parade. It was followed by the Dibs High School marching band, dozens of little kids on bicycles, a clown nobody remembered hiring, and five of the high school's six cheerleaders, Jennie Lou having been overcome by nausea in fearful anticipation of her upcoming modeling stint. Bringing up the rear was a representation of every roundup club in the county, and behind them, the cleanup crew.

Jennie Lou revived in time to walk the runway, and the Carters enthusiastically applauded, relieved that God hadn't stricken down their entire family when their daughter appeared in the garb of a man. But it was Melba who stole the show and Roy's heart, though not necessarily in that order. Clarissa took one look at Melba walking the runway with flair in her fantastic pantsuit and ordered a dozen larger sized outfits in assorted colors and styles for herself. At last! A line of clothing that could make a fat girl look as good as she felt, and Clarissa felt very good indeed. She had no idea that Helga was already calling her newest line of clothing Big Is Beautiful, or that Melba had accidentally named the line herself.

―――※―――

By eight-thirty that morning, Sorrells had parked in Marston's driveway. He reached into the glove box, removed a revolver, slid out of the car with the gun in his belt and walked onto the porch.

"Mr. Marston," he called out as he knocked on the door. "Mr. Marston, I'm Captain Warren from Ft. Sill. I have an important message for you."

Marston opened the door and blinked in the bright light. "A message?" he said, and then he saw the gun. "Oh my God!" Sorrells pushed Marston back into the living room. He was shaking. "What do you want?" he rasped. "I don't have any money!"

"Marston, I'm going to need your complete attention."

"Listen to me, whoever you are," Marston whimpered. "You should leave now. I won't call the police. Just … just go."

Marston was used to getting his way, but he wasn't going to win this one. Sorrells kicked him in the groin and he fell to the floor. He kicked him again, this time in the ribs as he rolled in agony on the floor. Then he pulled him to his feet, but only long enough to throw him over a lamp table and into a wall. When Marston slid to the floor, he grabbed him by the hair and pulled his face to within inches of his own. "I can do this all day," Sorrells said. "Is that what you want?"

Through dull eyes, Marston stared at his tormentor in disbelief. "What ... what do you want me to do?" he gasped.

"Get your ass over there and sit down," Sorrells said, gesturing toward the breakfast nook. "You're going to write something." Marston struggled to his feet and did as he was told. Sorrells placed a sheet of paper on the table, produced the pen and ink from his pocket, and set them in front of Marston. Then he unfolded a document he had prepared the night before. "Now," he said, "I'm going to read this to you and you write it exactly as I'm telling you. Otherwise we'll go back to me beating you to death. Do you understand?"

Marston nodded. "Yes," he said. "I understand." He filled the pen with a shaking hand, and Sorrells began to read from his notes. "I, John Marston, hereby give to my wife, Helga. ..."

Marston's head jerked up. "Why are you doing this?" he asked. "What are you to Helga?" Are you the boyfriend Les Jones told me about?"

Sorrells pulled the revolver from his belt, cocked it and put the barrel against Marston's ear. "Les Jones is dead. I killed him."

Marston picked up the pen and wrote as Sorrells dictated from his notes. "I, John Marston, hereby give to my wife, Helga Heinke Marston, all my interest in the Marston Ranch located three miles east of Dibs, Oklahoma, on County Line Road."

When he finished, Sorrells examined what Marston had written, folded the paper and put it in an envelope.

"Okay, now, let's get you dressed." He followed Marston into the bedroom. He probably didn't have a weapon, but it was better to be careful. Sorrells sat on the edge of the bed while Marston's trembling fingers fumbled with buttons and buckles.

"You know, John," Sorrells said later as he was enjoying a cup of coffee from Marston's pot, "this whole thing is different than I planned. I came here to kill you." He paused before continuing, "And yet, here you are, still alive."

"Why would you want to kill me? What have I ever done to you?"

"Oh, hell, John, that's an easy question. You just piss me off. Now what you need to think about is how to keep me from changing my mind again."

Sorrells looked at his watch. It was nine-thirty. "We've got about thirty minutes to kill, so I'm going to tell you how to assure yourself of a long life. First, you will never, I mean never, go anywhere near Mrs. Marston again. You will cause her no more difficulties of any kind. Do you understand?

Marston nodded. "You know that the ranch is mortgaged. Your name will still be on that paper, but unless you show your face anywhere around Dibs, she will make the payments. Any other debts you may owe are your problem. Mrs. Marston isn't involved.

"This paper you just wrote and are going to sign does exactly what you wanted when you left your wife and creditors behind, which was to be shut of the whole deal. So the way I see it, everybody gets what they want. You can start a new life or stay here and continue screwing the wives of men serving their country, although I'll tell you that really upsets me."

"How did you know about that?" Marston asked.

"John, John, I know more about you than I want to know. Two more things, John. In a little while we'll get in my car and go have the document you signed witnessed. That means walking into a business establishment where you are known and asking two people to sign as witnesses of your signature.

"You'll think you might be able to do something to stop that from happening. That would be a mistake, because I'll kill you on the spot. No one will even try to stop me from walking out. Only you have any idea who I am, and you will be dead. Do you understand that?" John nodded.

"The last thing I want you to understand is that you have been very lucky here today, at least so far. Lucky that my friend, who is a better man than I deserve for a friend, would grieve if I killed you. That's pretty much why you're still alive.

"Now let me tell you again where all this is going. If I ever hear of you bothering your soon-to-be ex-wife again, in any way whatsoever, I promise that regardless of my friend, I will hunt you down and kill you. There will be none of this bullshit conversation. You most likely won't even see me, but you will surely die."

Marston nodded.

"Good. Let's take a drive."

Marston sat silently as Sorrells pulled up in front of the Horny Toad. When they climbed out of the Ford, Sorrells turned to Marston, "You should have worn your Hawaiian shirt, John, you'd feel right at home."

They walked into the Horny Toad. The same bartender Sorrells had met the other night was washing glasses, stacking them on racks behind the bar. Another man was sweeping the floor. Sorrells pushed Marston forward.

"Hi. My friend here has something that requires two witnesses. You and your cleanup man mind helping him out?"

It took all of ten minutes. Sorrells drove Marston back to his house and pulled into the driveway.

"Well, John, it looks like we're done here." Sorrells slid the revolver from his belt and delivered a hammer blow to Marston's face, breaking his nose, before he opened the glove box and pushed the gun inside.

"Don't bleed on the upholstery," he said as Marston fumbled for the door handle.

"Oh, and, John. You asked me about my relationship with Mrs. Marston? I'm her hired hand."

Chapter Thirty
Charlie's Birthday

His business concluded, Sorrells lost no time in leaving Lawton. He needed to get the document he had obtained from Marston into Helga's hands, but he had no intention of returning to the ranch. He would leave it with Eli Steigner.

Later that Thursday afternoon, he parked in front of the Lutheran Church in Woodson. There were a couple of cars parked on the grounds, one of which he recognized as Eli's. He was not surprised to find the church door open. No one ever bothered to lock the doors to a church in towns like this one.

Although he did not consider himself a religious man, on the few occasions he had been inside a church, he had experienced a sense of wellbeing and peace. That was particularly true today when the church was devoid of worshipers and he was alone.

He had been sitting in one of the pews for about twenty minutes when Eli Steigner found him there and sat down beside him. Neither said a word for some time. Then Sorrells turned to his friend and said, "I've got something I want you to take to Helga Marston." He reached inside his shirt and passed the envelope to Steigner. "You need to open it."

"You got this from John Marston?" Eli said as he examined the document.

"I did."

"And Marston ..."

"He's alive and in reasonably good condition," Sorrells replied, recognizing his friend's concern. There was a hint of a smile on his face. "Thanks to you," he added as he stood to leave.

"Why don't you take it to Helga?" Steigner asked.

"I'm done there," Sorrells said, turning to the door. "If I go back, it will just complicate her life and mine too."

Steigner followed him to the door. "You could change. In fact I think you have."

"What makes you say that?"

"John Marston is still alive," were Eli's final words as Sorrells walked to his car.

Eli returned to the pew he and Sorrells had occupied and asked God to help Jake Sorrells. Then he went home to call Helga.

"Jake Sorrells was here," he said. "He left something for you. I'd like to bring it to you tomorrow if that's possible."

It was late when the Reverend called. Helga was exhausted from the day's celebration but she was determined to wait up for Charlie to get home from the dance. Now she was wide awake, puzzling over what the Reverend might be bringing her from Sorrells the next day. All things considered, she doubted she would get much sleep that night, but a great calm came over her when she saw the car lights shine into the yard. She hadn't realized how concerned she had been about Charlie at the wheel of an unfamiliar car. Waiting up for him was another thing she vowed not to start. He deserved something better than a worrywart of a mother. She turned off the bedside lamp and turned over on her side. It was the last turn she would make before morning.

The wind had kicked up by the time Reverend Steigner and his wife arrived at the ranch where Helga, in anticipation of their visit, was preparing dinner. Immediately, Steigner removed the envelope from the inside pocket of his jacket and handed it to her.

"What is it?" she asked.

"Open it."

Helga read the document, astounded that John Marston would ever write such a thing. "Why did he do this?" she asked.

"Sorrells asked him to, I suppose. As you can see, he has deeded his interest in the ranch to you."

The wind peppered pellets of sand against the windowpanes. Not a serious wind yet. Maybe this one would wear itself out before it turned into a full-blown sand storm.

She thoughtfully placed the deed on the table. "And John? What of him?"

"Jake told me he survived their discussion, and I thank God for that. Let's sit down. I have something I'd like you to consider."

Helga poured coffee and carried their cups to the table.

"This deed doesn't mean your troubles with John are over," he said, "but it's a start. I'm sure Jake asked him to stay away, but knowing him as we do, he might change his mind. You're making the ranch pay, and Mary here tells me you're clothing business is prospering. That might work against you."

"Then what should I do?" Helga asked.

"Throughout my years in the ministry, there have been only a handful of times when I've offered the advice I'm about to offer you. Clearly, you need to file for a divorce as soon as possible."

Helga nodded in agreement. "You're right. I should have done that a long time ago."

Mary covered Helga's hand with hers and said, "Eli and I don't want you to suffer anymore at the hands of John Marston, dear. Please do as my husband suggests. Rid yourself of that despicable man. There's a lawyer in our church. A good man. Eli will ask him to help you if you will agree to it."

Not trusting herself to speak, Helga nodded her assent after which, as if on cue, Charlie and Pup came bursting into the house, accompanied by a sandy blast of wind. He had recognized the Steigners' car and anticipated a visit with his friend the Reverend. Besides, it was suppertime, and he and Pup were both hungry. Helga contributed to the conversation throughout the meal, but she kept the deed next to her plate and her thoughts were on Jake. This was the last thing he would ever do for her, and she wouldn't know how to thank him even if she knew where to find him.

As Charlie prepared for bed, his thoughts took a different track. He was, after all, just a kid, and as much as he missed Sorrells, sometimes he thought he might miss his pickup even more.

Tomorrow was his birthday. He had waited sixteen years for a license to drive, and now, with the pickup gone, there was no use in having one. He would have to rely on Helga, and with her business requiring her to be gone so much, there would be little driving for him. One of the Mason boys would have to take him into Woodson for school supplies, and he'd probably have to drive the old flatbed truck to take the high school re-entrance exam Monday, if that's what the superintendent asked him to do. When Charlie considered the possibility that he would be riding the bus to school throughout the next year, he was tempted to flunk the exams on purpose.

When Sorrells drove away from the Woodson Lutheran Church, he had no idea how far a day's drive might take him. Breakdowns had always been a consideration in his old pickup. Now all the stops for oil and water weren't necessary, and he seemed to fly down the highway.

Without thinking, he drove west into New Mexico, then turned north into Colorado. He had grown accustomed to the flat, dry land of Western Oklahoma and hadn't realized how much he missed the mountains and the cool air that flowed down from their peaks.

He crossed over the Colorado border skirting the eastern edge of the San Juan range. When his mind drifted back to the ranch, to Charlie and to Helga, he forced himself to think of other things. One of the advantages his earlier work and lifestyle provided was an unlimited freedom of movement. He could call Bob Philpot to see if any work might be available, but he resisted the idea, at least for the present.

That evening he pulled off the road at Pagosa Springs and spent the night in the car, but he was back on his way by sunup Friday morning, driving north. When he stopped for breakfast at a café in Wolf Creek Pass, he noticed a sign posted by the door.

"Help wanted," it read. "Dependable man needed for seasonal work at Beamon's Fish Camp. Housing furnished. Apply in person. Beamon's Fish Camp, Beaver Creek Reservoir."

He pulled the notice from the wall and asked the waitress for directions. It was hardly the work he was accustomed to, but the idea of a month or two in the mountains appealed to him. It might be a place where he could limit his contact with others.

A few miles further up the road, he turned into Beaver Creek Reservoir and followed a winding road up to Beamon's Fish Camp where a dozen small, rustic cabins nestled in a semi-circle facing the lake. A larger structure was set off to the side near a dock that reached out over the clear water of the mountain lake, and two smaller docks had canoes and a few johnboats tied to them. A sign on the larger building read: Office and Store.

Inside, a youngish woman was restocking the shelves that lined the walls. She smiled pleasantly as Sorrells came through the door.

"Have you filled this job?" he said, holding up the notice he had taken from the café.

Before she could answer, a man in a wheelchair pushed through the door of the office behind the counter. "Hi," he said, "my name's Mack Beamon. This is my wife, April." Sorrells and the Beamons exchanged handshakes, and then, "No," Beamon said, "we haven't filled the position. I'm assuming you're interested?"

"I think so," Sorrells said.

"It's a three-months' job, you know. April and I will be back home in Arizona before the first blizzard blows in. I'm glad to see a full-grown man apply. Some see the job as a chance to sell a little bait, maybe clean up the camp site, then drink all weekend. Actually, it's pretty much a seven day a week job, and that stops them dead in their tracks."

"That'd be okay with me," Sorrells replied. "I've got no place I need to go."

"Any family?" Mrs. Beamon asked.

"No, ma'am, just me."

"Come back to the office, Mr. Sorrells. Let's see if we can work this out." Mack pushed his wheelchair toward the office and Jake followed, impressed by the man's agility. Their business was conducted in minutes, and Mack followed him out to the car.

"You can pick the cabin you want," he said. "They're all the same."

"Did you hire him?" asked April when he returned.

"Yes, I did, and I don't think I'll be sorry. No reason. I just like the looks of him."

"Did he tell you anything about himself?"

"Not much. He's pretty closed mouth," and then he added, "he was in the war."

"Did he tell you that?"

"No, he didn't have to. I could tell."

Sorrells chose the first cabin he came to. It wasn't locked. He would learn later that none of them were. He made a mental note to ask the Beamons for a key. After carrying his possessions into the cabin, he returned to the store.

Mack rolled himself down a ramp attached to the porch and took Sorrells on a quick tour of the camp. Knowing that people with handicaps often resent offers of help when performing normal activities, Jake didn't interfere. Several canoes were lying across short sawhorses on the side of the trail leading to the dock. "That's my main job," Beamon said with a laugh. "Somebody's always poking a hole in one of them. We've got a few johnboats, so I'm getting to be a pretty good small engine mechanic, too."

"I notice that none of the cabins are occupied," Sorrells said. "Why's that?"

"We don't open till the weekend. They'll be full by then." Beamon pointed to a row of small outboard engines on a shortened workbench. "You a mechanic?"

"Yeah, I get by."

"Good, you take over that. I have a hell of a time moving them around."

Beamon was right. Friday night saw every cabin rented and several tents set up in the camping area near the pinewoods. Mack seemed to know every occupant, but he assured Jake he did not. Beamon was a people person, joking and laughing with all the fishermen as well as with Sorrells, who wished he were more like him.

Charlie's worries had been all for naught. That evening after the Steigners drove off into the building sand storm, Ned Osment drove onto the Marston place in Sorrells' pickup. But it had changed. Gone were the faded paint, the dented fenders and the torn seats. The truck had been repainted a bright yellow and the tires had been replaced by wide, white sidewalls, including the spare mounted on the side of the bed.

Charlie came out of the bunkhouse and into the swirling sand to stand looking on in silence, a reaction Ned hadn't expected. He couldn't have known he had made his delivery the day before Charlie's sixteenth birthday, or that the boy was struggling to balance his emotions between unmanly tears and jumping for joy, which was what Pup was doing at his feet.

Ned rambled on, confused by Charlie's silence. "Jake dropped it off the other day," he said. "Told me to bring it out when I had it finished. Said you'd be need'n it. Looks good if I do say so. Runs good too."

Charlie ran his hand over the bright new paint. There was reverence in his voice when he said, "It sure does!" Then he saw the radio antenna rising from the right fender, and any trace of reserve melted in that instant. "It's got a radio!" he shouted. "A radio!"

"That's right," Ned said, a smile of pride spreading across his face. The boy approved of his work. It was going to be okay. Ned snickered. "Jake said you'd need that when you went out court'n the girls," he said. "And lookie here." He opened the door and ran a hand over the seat covers. "They's them new plastic ones."

"Mom!" Charlie hollered back toward the house, but his eyes remained glued to the miracle parked before him, the gift from a man he idolized. "Mom, come see what Jake gave me for my birthday. Come quick! He didn't forget!"

Helga had witnessed the events unfolding out front amidst the swirling sand from the moment Ned had driven the pickup into the yard. After Charlie's third "Mom!" rang out, she remained hidden behind the front room curtain only long enough to get control of herself before hurrying out to join him.

"Evenin, Mrs. Marston," said Ned, but Helga raced past him to throw her arms about an embarrassed Charlie.

"Happy birthday," she said, then quickly released him. "Looks like the paint job on my own car will be safe now," Helga quipped.

"You'll be taking your drivers test in your own vehicle tomorrow, but we'd best get it into the barn with mine before the sand eats the paint job off it."

Ned cleared his throat. "Uh, say, Ma'am, reck'n Charlie could give me a ride back to the garage first?"

"You bet I could!" Charlie said. "Hop aboard."

He held out his hand, Ned placed the keys in it and Charlie's manhood was secure.

Chapter Thirty-One
Fishing Camp

Windstorms weren't uncommon in the northwestern corner of Oklahoma no matter the season. They came without warning, went on till they wore themselves out, and left as abruptly as they had come. The wind continued to howl throughout that Friday evening and went on until daylight, whipping the sandy terrain into eddies, burying small pieces of equipment carelessly left in the yard and uncovering others buried by the last windstorm. This time the capricious wind stilled before morning, and Saturday dawned bright and calm. Fortunately, Charlie's pickup was parked safely beside Helga's car in the barn. The sand that drifted in mounds a third of the way up the fence posts had the power to grind the paint off a car all the way down to the frame.

Charlie scooped away the sand drift in front of the door and, whistling an unidentifiable tune, entered the house behind Pup, who bounded joyfully about the kitchen in response to Charlie's mood.

"Happy birthday!" Helga called over her shoulder from where she stood at the stove flipping the blueberry hot cakes Charlie had ordered for his birthday breakfast. "Happy sixteenth!" she amended as she set the steaming plate before him, resisting the temptation to muss his carefully combed hair. She rightly assumed he would be feeling the dignity of his years this morning, and she must remember to respect that. Helga silently congratulated herself on how wise she had grown to the ways of teenaged boys in the past months. Charlie truly was on the top of his world this morning. He had taken the prettiest girl in the county to the street dance Thursday night, and she had agreed to go to the movies with him tonight. He could hardly wait to see the expression on her face when he drove up in his very own bright yellow pickup, a fully licensed and legal driver at last. He might put his arm around her in the dark theater if they sat far enough toward the back. But only if she leaned into him just a little to let him know it was all right.

Everything depended on his passing both the written and the driving test this morning. Helga would accompany him to Woodson and wait in the lobby while he took the written test and then the actual driving test itself. After that, they would shop for school clothes and the birthday gift Helga said he could choose at any store in town. He knew exactly what he wanted and where to get it, so the gift would be a bigger surprise to her than to him.

He felt reasonably confident about the written test he would be taking in a couple of hours. He had picked up the drivers manual at the post office when Jake started teaching him to drive. The manual had been his constant companion ever since, sometimes tucked inside the literature book he was supposed to be reading. His friends had warned him of certain pitfalls he might encounter in the driving test, including parallel parking, but that wouldn't be a problem. Dibs streets didn't require that kind of parking, but he had spent hours executing the necessary maneuvers out in the pasture between barriers he had set up for that purpose. Charlie believed in being prepared.

If he had been going to be nervous about driving on the highway to Woodson for the first time with his mom sitting beside him, Helga took care of that. She unfolded an enormous sketchpad in her lap, produced a charcoal pencil, bent her head over her work, and didn't say a word until they crossed Woodson's city limits. "Oh!"

she exclaimed, closing the tablet, "are we here already?" If Charlie had glanced at the sketchpad, he would have seen erratic doodling rather than the fashion design he supposed she was creating. Helga had anticipated the tension of the situation, both his and hers, and contrived a plan to set them both at ease. She, too, believed in being prepared.

An hour and a half later, an officer came into the courthouse lobby where Helga pretended to read. "Your boy did a fine job," he said. "Farm kids usually do. Most of 'em have been driving since they were big enough to see over the steering wheel, but your boy can parallel park, too. That's unusual. You got a fine son here. He missed the one on the written test about the distance behind the car in front, but that's the only one."

Helga's mother heart was big when Charlie appeared in the doorway flashing the drivers license he had been issued. They descended the narrow stairs single file to the sidewalk, where she threw an arm across his shoulders and let him lead the way to the pickup. He had reached the driver's side before he heard her clear her throat and noticed that she was standing on the passenger side glancing about vaguely, humming a little tune, waiting for him to open the door for her. He immediately rushed around to her side, opened the door and helped her inside. She patted his arm as he reached for the ignition and smiled. "Remember that tonight when you pick up Jennie Lou," she said. "If she's not impressed, her parents will be."

Helga was mystified when Charlie pulled up in front of the Western Auto store, hurried around to open her door and, with a nod of his head, indicated his intention for them to go inside. Her first impression was that the place could use some organizing. Pressure cookers nestled against bicycle tires, and bins of nails and screws were separated from small auto parts by shelves where all manner of lubricants and motor oil were stored. Charlie knew where he was going. He walked straight to a ceiling-high case at the side of the building, reached up to a top shelf and brought down a genuine leather Wilson football.

"This is it?" Helga asked, relieved that she hadn't bungled into getting him a Parker pen and pencil set or some other such useless gift. "This is what you want for your birthday?" Charlie nodded and she laughed, puzzled by his selection but pleased. "You're just full of surprises, aren't you?" she said. "Well, come along then, we'll see if we can find someone to wait on us. A football for goodness sake." She continued to ramble on as she looked about for a clerk. "It never occurred to me you'd be interested in sports, but why wouldn't you be? I suppose all high school boys are. Even younger, I imagine, but...

"Oh, there you are," she said when she spotted the thin young man who appeared behind the counter. "I want to pay for the football my son is holding, please." Charlie and the clerk exchanged knowing grins as money changed hands, and then Helga followed her amused but self-controlled teen-ager out of the store. She had been a mother less than a week. She had a lot to learn, but she already loved it.

Charlie suggested they walk to J.C. Penney's for his school clothes, but Helga had once again planned ahead. "Huh uh," she said. "Let's drive." They found a parking place near the double doors and located the men and boys' clothing section, where Helga took a seat in a leather chair.

Throughout the next half hour or so she proceeded to nod or shake her head at the selections Charlie brought out for her approval. A mound of levis and shirts was growing when he presented her with a pink, French cuffed dress shirt. Helga's eyebrows flew up. She frowned and vigorously shook her head before she saw that he was grinning. "Just checking," he said, "making sure you were paying attention."

In the end, they were both grateful that Charlie had found a parking place just outside the door because it took both of them to get their purchases transferred to the bed of the pickup, and there was barely enough room for the school supplies they picked up at TG&Y. "How about stopping for a root beer before we leave town?" Helga suggested. "I'm bushed."

It was suppertime by the time they reached Clem's Café, where Melba had insisted they stop on their way home. "It won't take long," she had said in her early morning phone call. "The movie doesn't start till eight. Charlie'll have plenty of time to run out to the ranch and clean up before he picks up Jennie Lou, and I've got a surprise that won't wait."

Roy and Melba sat with their heads together in the largest booth, where they were making notes on a tablet lying on the table. A good many of the lines written there had been crossed out and notations made above them. "What do you think, Pop?" Melba called out to her dad in the kitchen. "Roy doesn't want us to crowd you, but he thinks we should leave that up to you."

Clem stuck his head through the serving window in time to see Charlie and Helga walk in. "Here's the birthday boy and his mom," he said. "I'll get his burger on the grill and we'll discuss your housing options while he eats. Happy birthday, Charlie. I'll be out in a minute."

"Oh, hi!" exclaimed Melba, moving the tablet aside as Helga and Charlie approached. "Charlie, you scoot in there beside Roy. Helga, sit here beside me. We've got decisions to make, and we need help."

It had been going on like that between the two of them ever since Roy popped the question, and for a while it looked like tension would scuttle the wedding altogether. Helga sided with Roy when he suggested a civil ceremony and maybe a small reception later, but Melba seemed bent on a no-holds-barred blowout at the church. Helga kept waiting for Roy to put his foot down and was disappointed in him when he didn't. There was no doubt that he was crazy about Melba, but his plan made more sense, and it wasn't like him to let anyone run over him.

"What's the issue now?" Helga asked, reaching across both of them to snitch one of Charlie's French fries. "Last time it was whether to have four or six bridesmaids, and the time before that it was a toss up between roses and gardenias. We're all sick of this wedding and it hasn't even come off yet and probably won't unless. ..."

Roy and Melba looked like the proverbial cat who had swallowed the proverbial canary. Clem beamed at them from the counter where he kept an eye out for customers. "They took care of that this morning," he said, handing Helga a handful of rice. "Go ahead. Anoint the bride and groom and let's get on with the list they're making now.

"No, Roy, you ain't going to be crowding me none when you move into the house. I wouldn't be easy any other way. Store whatever you want of your own in the shed out back, bring on inside whatever you need or want, and park out front alongside my heap. Fact is, I'll feel safer with you inside the house, and I know Melba will too. Among other reasons," he added with a twinkle before he shuffled off to take care of the couple sitting on the other side of the room.

Immediately, Helga and Mable and Roy were in the midst of a group hug, then Charlie and Roy and Melba, and then there were one on one hugs until everyone felt thoroughly congratulated. Finally, the ring was admired all around, and the happy couple blushed in pride and confusion. "A wedding should be a beautiful, private thing," Helga said before they took their leave. "Congratulations, Mr. and Mrs. Roy Strange. You couldn't have pulled it off better."

Only Charlie saw her look of longing as he drove them home.

Throughout his first two weeks at Beamon's Fish Camp on the Beaver Creek Reservoir, Jake and Mack developed an unspoken bond. Mack never pried, but he was so open about himself that Jake came to trust him. He too had a history of experience with military hospitals.

"It was in the South Pacific," Mack told him in the third week of their acquaintance. "One of those damn crazy Kamikazes dropped right down on top of my ship. I was the only man alive anywhere near the explosion. Blew me across the ship. Anyway, I figured I was a dead man. You ever hear anything like that? I mean thinking you're dead? Truth is, I still sometimes do."

Sorrells didn't answer.

"Anyway, I spent the duration in the hospital and rolled out of it in one of these things." He patted the arms of his chair.

"You ever have dreams about it?" Sorrells asked.

"You mean like nightmares and cold sweats?"

"Yeah."

"Used to. All the time."

"Not any more?" Sorrells asked.

"Funny thing about that. April and I had a kind of agreement before I shipped out. After this — Beamon patted the chair again — I figured there was no way, but she wanted to get married anyway, God bless her. It wasn't long before I somehow quit worrying about the stuff I couldn't do anything about and concentrated on building a life with April. The nightmares went away."

"I still have them," Sorrells said.

"Do they ever go away?"

"Once. They went away once."

Neither of them pursued the issue further. Jake went about his work, the hours melding into days and the days into weeks. For the most part, Sorrells enjoyed the work, the lake and the mountains, but he felt himself slipping back into his darker side. The dreams were coming more frequently now, and thoughts of the peace alcohol would bring made whiskey almost irresistible.

The Beamons recognized what was happening and felt compelled to help. "Look, Jake," Mack said one day when Jake was nearing the bottom, "I need you. I can't handle this place without help, and it's too late to get anybody else. You told me you don't drink on the job. Well, this is your job. April and I want you sober, and believe me when I tell you, you're headed for a bender. I know the signs. As I see it, you've got two choices. You can get your ass out of here, or you can let me help you. But if you run, don't ever tell yourself that your drinking didn't affect anyone but yourself, because you'll be leaving April and me high and dry."

"What's the other choice?"

"You let us help you. I've been through this myself and I know how tough it is, but I did it with April's help, and you can too."

Throughout the next three days and four nights, Mack stayed in Sorrells' cabin with him. At first he resented Mack's attempts to help. Just more of the same thing Eli Steigner and the VA Hospital had tried to do, he told himself. When he became agitated and struck out verbally, Beamon gave it back to him in kind. Other times, they talked. Never had Jake Sorrells bared his soul to another human being as he did to this man who had overcome what he himself was enduring now.

They talked about the war; the hospital; the drinking, and, in the end, Mack's relationship with April and the short time Jake had spent with Helga Marston.

One evening Mack said, "Jake, you said that once the dreams went away."

Jake nodded.

"Were you with Helga when the dreams stopped?"

Jake nodded again.

"Well, you dumb SOB, doesn't that tell you something?"

"I'm no good for her," Jake said softly. "Maybe she thought she needed me then, but. ... "

"Aw, bullshit, Jake, what the hell do you know about how

women think? I'm washing my hands of you. From now on you're going to be dealing with April!" And that's when Mack's wife took over.

Chapter Thirty-Two
Tough Times

"Uncontested." Helga read the document again to be sure before she phoned Melba. "It came in the mail today!" Helga shouted into the receiver. "John signed the papers! They're right here in my hand."

"Take a deep breath and slow down," said Melba. "You've had the documents showing that John's name was officially removed from the deed to the ranch for almost a month now. What papers are you talking about?"

"Divorce papers, Melba. Divorce! I'm a free woman. What a lovely lawyer Reverend Steigner set me up with. I'm going to send him flowers, and. ..."

"Wait up, my friend," said Melba in her reasoning voice. "Oklahoma law requires a six months waiting period before the divorce is final."

"Meaning what?" asked a more subdued Helga.

Melba laughed. "Meaning you can't remarry before then."

"As though I'd want to!" exclaimed Helga, and then they were both laughing. "Let's have a party," she said, "or at least share a bottle of wine."

"Okay, but not till the weekend. "Dad's going to rebel if I leave him here to ramrod the help alone again. You divorced women might have time for fun and frivolity, but we married women have responsibilities."

Nothing could have been further from the truth. Helga's weekdays started before dawn when she put breakfast on the table for Charlie and the Mason boys and sat down to go over the day's schedule with them before seeing Charlie off to school. She suspected he would like to go out for football, but he never mentioned it. For him, the ranch came first. For her, Charlie came first, and she would somehow see that he got that chance next year. Thank goodness Sid and Fred had agreed to move into the bunkhouse with Charlie when Jake left. The ranch continued to be a profitable business, but it required all of the Mason boys' time and effort to continue the program Jake had put in place.

Charlie hit it hard after school and on weekends, but he needed time for his studies, and Helga insisted he get a good night's sleep. She enjoyed helping out at the ranch when her schedule allowed, but she regularly spent half of every day in Dibs. The guild ladies were talented and dependable and the fashion business was doing well; but they lacked the direction only she could give them, and they needed her encouragement.

Helga welcomed the busy schedule that had kept her mind occupied throughout the months since Jake left. In the evenings, if the boys didn't need her help in the fields or barn, she left a salad in the refrigerator and a casserole in the oven, saddled Miss Bess, and the two of them flew over pastureland to the pond. Strange, she thought, that the pond would be the place where she felt closest to Jake. Sometimes it seemed as though she could reach out and touch him, but her hand brushed against the rough bark of her leaning tree and came back to her empty. Those were not the good days. The good days came on weekends when Charlie and Pup joined her there for a picnic. They talked about Jake, wondered aloud where he was, what he was doing, and if he thought about them. They remembered the bad days when Jones died trying to kill them all and the good days when Jake taught them to work cattle, and they agreed that the good days far outweighed the bad. At those times, Sorrells was there with them in spirit. They felt it. They knew it, and they left the pond with renewed faith that he would one day return to them.

Then came the Saturday when they returned from the pond to find the Mason boys sitting in their pickup, their duffel bags thrown onto the bed. Helga and Charlie had ridden their horses into the yard and dismounted before first Sid and then Fred got out of the cab and turned to face them.

"Mrs. Marston," said Sid, "I'm awful sorry to leave you in a fix, but we got our papers this morning. I joined the National Guard along with the other guys in my class right out of high school, and so did Fred. They've called up the 45th Division. That's both of us. Probably all of us. We'll be heading out for camp next week to train for a stint in Korea."

Helga smiled a frozen smile and nodded her head.

"Dad thinks he can help you out on weekends, and he says there's others he knows who can help now and then, but that's not like having steady help."

"Come in the house, boys," said Helga. "I'm proud of you. Charlie will put the horses up and join us. We'll be in the kitchen, Charlie, getting around a cherry pie. I was saving it for tomorrow, but this is a special occasion."

Her heart beat a wild tattoo and the palms of her hands were clammy, but she was relieved to hear her voice come out strong, almost cheerful. How could she do without these fine, steady young men who faithfully did all the work the ranch required. How could Ed and Elsie and all the other Dibs mothers and fathers let their boys go? How would she be able to let Charlie go if such orders were to one day come for him?

Sid and Fred seemed more at ease by the time Charlie walked

with them to their pickup. Helga remained seated at the table, so deep in thought that she didn't hear Charlie come back inside. He laid a hand on her shoulder and bent down to meet her gaze.

"It's okay, Mom," he said, flashing a smile that neither of them believed. "I'll get back into school next year when this Korea thing is over and hired help is. ..."

"No!" Helga all but exploded, "quitting school is the one thing you won't do. The entire community will be ranching shorthanded now that so many of our young men have been called up, but we'll make it. All you and I need is each other and a plan, and I think I have one. The guild ladies can handle the work in town. They lack confidence, but they'll soon see that they can make it without me. I'll drop by for an hour or so a couple mornings throughout the week, and I'll see that the orders get to the post office, but that's all. You and I will keep things running here. Maybe not as well with just two of us, but we can do it. I know we can."

Time proved Helga right. The guild ladies valued the faith Helga placed in them and rose to the occasion. Charlie might have worn an un-ironed shirt to school a time or two, but he didn't miss a day. If anything, their relationship strengthened as they worked side by side in the evenings, and sometimes on into the night, finishing up what Helga hadn't finished in daylight hours. More often than not, they fell into bed exhausted, but they rose refreshed at dawn to welcome the challenge they faced together.

Chapter Thirty-Three
Sorrells Has Friends

Back at the fishing camp, Jake Sorrells and April Beamon had squared off and come out swinging. Their conversations started off pleasantly enough, but she took her job seriously, and it wasn't long before he knew he had met his match.

"Your problem isn't Helga's problem," April yelled.

"I know that!" Sorrells yelled back.

"Listen to me, you dumb oaf! I'm saying this is your problem, not hers, but, God help her, she could be the solution. Look at you, Jake Sorrells. By your own admission, you go through life with only one close friend, that preacher. Then when somebody tries to love you, like that kid, Charlie, you told Mack about and that woman on the ranch — you run like hell. Mack and I know it's possible to change. Change everything. But it's not going to happen when, every time someone gets close, you reject them. How many chances at happiness are going to come your way?"

"There are things about me, April, that you and Mack don't know. Things you couldn't imagine."

"Okay, fine. Change that too. Change your whole damn life! Lord knows you need to."

"I can't argue with that," Sorrells said with a half smile.

He had always known the drinking was only one of the symptoms of his greater problem. Once he conquered that, maybe he could work on the others. He'd need a new line of work, though. What he'd been doing before he reached the Marston ranch was also a symptom, but it would be a lot easier to overcome than his desire for liquor. Sorrells shrugged. Even if he cleaned up the symptoms, there'd still be that greater problem at the core.

The fall fishing season was about to end, and then Jake would be gone. The Beamons had undertaken a long-term project that began with five intense days. They believed they'd made progress, but their work was not over yet.

To his credit, Jake no longer objected to their attempts to help him. For once in his life he realized that help was a good thing. Otherwise he would have run. He didn't drink, either. He might have credited the mountain air or his new healthier lifestyle, but deep down he knew it was the friendship offered so willingly by the Beamons that was turning his life around.

Then one day the fishermen disappeared and the camp was every bit as deserted as it had been when Sorrells first saw it.

"Just in time," said Mack, adjusting the radio dial. "The weatherman is predicting an early snow. Everything on the place needs to be stored away or secured for the winter."

Sorrells set about shutting down the camp, and then suddenly there was no more to do. On his last day at the camp, he had a last cup of coffee with the Beamons. They shook hands and hugged, and then he stopped at the door, looked back and said, "Mack, you know, when I told you I only had one friend? Well, I know that's not the way things are now. I've got more friends than one. Thanks for everything."

"You've got friends in Oklahoma too," April yelled after him.

Sorrells raised an arm in acknowledgment but didn't look back when he yelled, "I was counting them." He smiled to himself as he headed for the car.

He stopped at a pay phone in Wolf Creek and called Bob Philpot. "Bob's out working a case, Jake," the secretary said. "He'll be sorry he missed you. Do you have a number. ..." Then she realized who she was talking to. "I'm sure you will need to call back."

"Just tell him I'm going to be out of pocket for awhile. I'm not taking any new jobs."

Sorrells' time at the Beamon's Fish Camp had given him a good start, and with it, a determination to change his life for the better. Out on the road, with nothing to do except watch the power poles whiz by, doubts began to fill his thoughts. He knew what he wanted, but would Helga feel the same way? When he first came to the ranch, she needed him. Now all of that had changed. With the successful clothing business she was building, why would she want to saddle herself with a man like him?

Other times he thought of what she and Charlie had given him. He hoped that somehow they had not given up on him. The miles seemed to drag by. Someone had once told him that the road home always seems longer. He didn't understand what that meant then, but he knew now. He was going home.

With the Mason brothers gone, Helga and Charlie struggled to keep the ranch running. Fortunately, the last cutting of hay was in the barn before Sid and Fred left. Any big projects would have to wait till extra help could be arranged. That might take time, but both Helga and Charlie believed they were up to the task. In the meantime, the cattle would need to be fed during the winter months. That would be their main concern.

There were no more extended breakfasts. At best, all they would have time for was cold cereal and orange juice or milk. Helga regretted having to give up the opportunity to lavish attention on Charlie. Attention she knew he needed. They were often together, but in the cab of the truck as she drove and Charlie in the back breaking open bales of hay for the cattle to eat. All this in the dark, before sunrise and after sunset, in good weather and bad, every day. When Charlie got home from school, the process continued. Helga tried to maintain a schedule with her business that allowed her to return to the ranch early enough to help Charlie fill the feed troughs with the high protein cubes that would enable the cows to bear strong, healthy calves in the early spring.

Charlie seemed to thrive on his newly acquired responsibility, believing, perhaps correctly, that he was accepting a man's place on the ranch, something he had not had when the Masons were there. He knew that Helga needed him. The ranch needed him.

Summer had ended with no rain in sight, and toward the end of September, the sandy earth was prone to shift about in the Oklahoma wind, making the early morning and late afternoon feedings even more troublesome than the shortage of time. The day came when Charlie had a student council meeting after school and would be late getting back. Helga, home from her work in Dibs, noticed the dust clouds building on the horizon and, pulling her kerchief up to cover her nose and mouth, she set out in hopes of getting the feed to the cattle in what little light remained before the sand storm reached the Marston place. Charlie had stacked feed sacks on the truck bed. It wouldn't be too difficult to pull them off and empty them into the wooden troughs.

The wind was nearing gale force as Helga began her drive across the ranch land. The cattle had already begun to crowd around the empty troughs in anticipation of her arrival. She filled four of the more distant troughs and would fill one more before she started working her way back.

The wind was now howling, and sand stung her face as she

labored to pull the feed sacks down from the truck and over to the troughs. While she struggled with the heavy sacks, her attention averted, the eager cattle pushed forward, catching her unaware and pinning her against the truck. The impact slammed her head against the truck bed, and she slumped to the ground in the choking sand, miraculously avoiding the animals' sharp hooves. She somehow managed to roll under the truck, where she lay drifting in and out of consciousness. In a lucid moment, she reasoned that if she could get to her feet and climb into the cab of the truck, even if she couldn't drive it, there was a chance she wouldn't suffocate in the choking sand.

When Charlie got home, he saw that the truck was gone and didn't pause before heading out in his pickup along the feed truck's ruts to help Helga with the feeding. When he finally saw the truck through the whirling sand, he was almost upon it. Lowing cattle were milling about the truck, but Helga was not in sight. "She should never have tried to do this by herself," he said aloud. "Not in this weather."

He drove up as close as he could, honking the horn to scatter the milling cattle, and trained the headlights on the truck. Helga was nowhere in sight, not in the bed of the truck and not in the cab. He tightened the bandana he'd tied over his mouth and nose and jumped out of the pickup calling her name, knowing she would never be able to hear him in the howling wind. Finally, he rolled beneath the truck and reached into areas where he could barely see, and his hand touched Helga's arm. When he called out her name, she stirred. Ranch work had made Charlie strong for a boy his age. He was able to pull her from beneath the truck and, partly carrying her and partly dragging her, he managed to get her into the pickup. She was conscious but gasping for air.

Charlie drove them back to the house and supported her as she stumbled inside. He helped her to the kitchen sink, where she cleared her eyes and throat of sand, and then Charlie began to rub her arms and legs to get the circulation going. He knew to put ice on a bruise, so he soaked a towel in ice water, folded it, and placed it on the knot that was growing larger on the side of her head. Soon the color of her skin had turned from a pale blue to its normal color and, though her voice was hoarse, she was talking. He wondered if he should call someone, but Helga said, "I wouldn't go back out in that dirt storm under any circumstances, and I wouldn't ask anyone to come here. Besides," she added with a faint smile, "you are nurse enough, Charlie. You're doing all anyone else could."

Helga was pretty much her normal self when she left Charlie to go to bed, but he would spend that night in the extra bedroom rather than leave her in the house alone. He might have felt a little twinge of jealousy when Pup chose to curl up at the foot of her bed.

Chapter Thirty-Four
Coming Home

On a Saturday afternoon not more than a couple of weeks after Helga's accident, Charlie drove into town to ask Jenny, who was working part-time at the dry goods store, if she would like to see the new Jimmy Stewart movie that night. Jimmy Stewart was a big deal to her, so he thought his chances were good, and they were. He knew her boss didn't like for her to visit while she was working, so he squeezed her hand and walked out onto the street. It wouldn't be long before he would see her again.

Back out on the street, he saw that someone was leaning against the driver's side of his pickup, and that wouldn't do! Nobody sat or leaned on his truck. Nobody. He had gone around to the passenger side and opened the door, intending to slide across the seat, when a familiar voice said, "You gett'n too damn high-toned to say hi to your old daddy, boy?"

Charlie was speechless. He hadn't heard his father's voice in more than a year. "Pretty good look'n pickup you got here," said Whit Conn. "You must be do'n pretty good for yourself, or did that German woman buy it for you? I hear you're living out there at the ranch with her. Well, I guess there ain't nothin' wrong with that, you being almost grown and all. God knows she's a good look'n bitch. What say I come out there for a visit? She might favor an older man with more experience for a change."

"Get your ass off my truck," Charlie shouted. "I never want to see you again. You got no call to talk that way about Mrs. Marston!" He started the pickup and roared away, his heart thumping and his mind racing. By no means was the man welcome back into his life, and then to be talking like that! He would have to be drunk to even think such a thing. Charlie had seen him drunk many times, and his mother too. Drunk or not, though, to say those things about the only person who had ever been a real mother to him, a woman he knew loved him as much as he loved her. There was just no call for that kind of talk. She and Jake had taken him in and made a place for him in their lives. Jake was gone, but he knew Helga would never desert him.

As he bounced over the rough road leading to the ranch, Charlie's thoughts turned to Jake. He needed him now more than ever. Jake would know what to do. Charlie had heard Reverend Steigner talk about the rage in Jake. How it exploded sometimes. For the first time in his life, Charlie believed he knew how that rage felt. As he neared the ranch, he started yelling out loud, "Why can't he just leave me alone! He never was a father to me. Both of them left me to get by any way I could. They didn't care what happened to me. Why would he come back now when everything is going so good?"

By the time he got to the ranch, he had decided not to tell Helga. There was no need to worry her about this. He would handle it himself. That's what Jake would do. The day before, Sorrells had phoned Eli Steigner from a gas station. "Eli, I'm headed your way," he said. "I'll be in Woodson sometime in the morning. I'd like to talk to you if you're going to be around."

"Good to hear from you, Jake, I'll be here. Does Helga know you're coming back?"

"No, she doesn't know, and I'd like to keep it that way."

"She would like to know."

"I've got some things to work out, Eli. Hold off on telling her at least till I get a chance to talk to you."

"I'm glad you're coming back, Jake. I'm looking forward to seeing you. ..." Sorrells had hung up.

He parked in front of the Lutheran Church late the next morning and walked into the church office. Eli stood, took the few steps the small office permitted, and put his arm around his friend's shoulders.

"How are they getting along?" Sorrells asked.

"Helga's business is doing great. Far better than could be imagined, and it's profiting the whole community. The ranch has been tougher since the Mason boys went off to war, but she and Charlie have hung on. He's growing like a weed and doing well in school. He's calling Helga 'Mom,' and she loves it. And, Jake, by the way, she's got her divorce. Now I want to hear about you. How are you getting along?"

"Better than you might think," he said, and then he told his friend about Mack and April Beamon, how they had refused to give up on him, and how he had eventually seen the light at the end of the tunnel.

Finally, when he had finished, Eli stood, clasped his hands together and said, "Praise God! He has answered my prayers."

"Maybe. I'm still working on it," Sorrells said.

"We're all still working on our lives, Jake. Now, can I call Helga?"

"I'm going to the ranch. I'll tell her myself. I've still got to see whether she would want me back in her life. I can sure see why she wouldn't."

"I think you will be pleasantly surprised at what her response will be," Eli said.

"I'll tell you one thing, Eli, I'm not going back to run a damn sewing machine."

Eli was still laughing as Jake left, but he caught up to him before he reached the curb, "Hey, Jake," he said, "I forgot to tell you that you won't be going back to the Marston Ranch. It's officially the Heinke Ranch now. When Helga reclaimed her maiden name, Roy and Melba presented her with the HH branding iron, so this spring's cattle will bear the Double H brand."

Thirty minutes later, Jake Sorrells was driving through Dibs toward the ranch, where Charlie had just finished loading the truck with sacks for the evening feeding. Helga was still in town tending to business, but she'd be back in time to help him. Charlie had loaded the last sack when he looked up to see a decrepit pickup parked beside the barn and Whit Conn walking out of the bunkhouse. "We didn't get finished with our talk," he said. "I figger it's time we get a few things worked out."

"We got nothing to say to each other. You showed me that in town. You need to get out'a here," Charlie said.

"That ain't no way to talk to me. I'm your daddy."

"That's nothing I'm apt to brag about," Charlie said.

"I guess you heard that no-account maw of yours up and run off with a damn truck driver 'bout a year ago. I don't get a hell-of-a-lot of respect out'a my family. I'm glad she's gone. She done me a favor. Her and her truck driver both, but you, boy, you got possibilities. I figger on gettin' at least a bit of a road stake out'a you."

"I don't have any money," Charlie said, "and if I did, I wouldn't give it to you."

"I didn't think you would, but that German woman of yours, I'll bet she would be damn glad to get shut of me for a price. Her stealing you away and all."

"Keep her out of this!" Charlie yelled. "Just get out of here. Leave us alone!"

"So it's like that, huh? Well, what say I just go up to the house and ask her my ownself?"

Whit had started toward the house, but Charlie blocked his way.

"Leave her alone," he said. "Besides, she's not home."

"Then I figger to wait till she's back. I ain't in no hurry. Besides, like I told you in town, she might like me better'n you do."

Whit was trying to move past him when Charlie grabbed his arm. "I told you to leave!"

"Get out'a my damn way, you worthless pup!" Whit hollered.

Neither of them heard Sorrells' car roll to a stop about fifty feet behind them, but Jake did see Charlie hit the man he was arguing with and knock him down. When he struggled to his feet, Charlie hit him again while Sorrells stood watching. He had the man by the collar and was dragging him toward an old pickup parked next to Sorrells' car when Charlie saw him.

"Have a little disagreement with this fellow, Charlie?" Jake asked.

"He's through here," Charlie answered, straining to lift Whit up off the ground.

"Let me help you," Sorrells said with a smile. "Now that you've convinced him, he's probably interested in getting on his way."

Sorrells raised the stranger up and pushed him into the old pick-up. "Fellow, my friend here was easy on you," said Jake. "I doubt it would be smart to come back." He slammed the door, then reached through the open window and slapped the stranger till his eyes opened. "Get your ass off this ranch," he said. "Do it now." And he did.

Now that the excitement was over, Charlie rushed to Sorrells and threw his arms around him. "Jake," he said, tilting his head to look into his eyes, "are you back?"

It was an important question, but Sorrells didn't answer. Instead he said, "Glad to see you, Charlie. Looks like you're pretty near grown now."

"Have you seen mom?" Charlie asked.

"Not yet. Who was the man you were having the discussion with?"

"He's my daddy, or he was once. Not anymore. I don't think we need to tell mom 'bout him coming back. She'd just worry."

"I think you're right. Besides, after what you did just now, my guess is you may be rid of him."

After Charlie told Sorrells about Helga's close call with the cattle, he asked, "Are you two running the place by yourselves?"

"Yeah, but since you're back. ... You are coming home aren't you?"

Sorrells put his hand on Charlie's shoulder. "Home? Well, I'd say your mom would have something to say about that, wouldn't you? Sounds like you would hire me back, but she might have another opinion."

"I know she would want you," said Charlie. "I just know! She loves you."

Sorrells didn't respond to his encouragement, but when Charlie jokingly told him he could have his storeroom back if he stayed, Sorrells said, "Regardless of whether I stay or not, if you need me for anything ... anything at all ... get in touch with Reverend Steigner. I'll make sure he always knows how to get in touch with me."

"Aw, Jake, please stay."

Sorrells couldn't meet his eyes. "I'm going to drive into town," he said. " I'll try to see Helga there."

Sorrells climbed into his Ford and had gotten as far as the gate before he came to his senses. "Aw, hell!" he said aloud as he turned the car around in the road. Charlie was waiting for him by the bunkhouse. "I'll help you feed the stock," Jake said.

When Helga arrived, she found an unfamiliar car parked near the barn. Must be one of Charlie's friends, she said to herself as she rushed into the house and quickly changed into her work clothes. While she waited in the barn for Charlie to get back, she broke open a couple of bales and put hay in the mangers for the horses. It was a nice day, she thought, considering what the recent weather had been. Cool, but not cold. The afternoon sun made the remaining hours of the day pleasant.

When she heard the truck approaching from the pasture, she stepped out of the barn to wave at Charlie. Yes, she'd been right. It appeared that one of his friends was with him. Or was that.... Could that be.... "Oh God! It's Jake."

Charlie got out of the truck, a wide grin across his face. "We got a place for a new hand, mom? I can teach him what he'll need to know."

Helga threw her arms around Jake, and he could feel her tears on his cheek. "Charlie," he murmured into the top of her head, "give us a little time to work things out, okay?"

"You bet!" Charlie said as he watched the two people he loved best walk toward the house arm in arm.

"Well, ma'am, what about it?" Jake asked once they were inside the door. "You up to hiring any new hands?"

"Just one," she replied. "But I've already got a man in mind for the job."

"Would that be me?"

"I suspect it would, but I can tell you it isn't a nine to five job. You'll be putting in a lot of extra hours."

"That sounds like something I can handle."

"Good. But if I hire you, there won't be any leaving just because you feel like moving on."

"I can handle that too. There's just one more thing."

"And that is?" Helga looked up at Jake.

"I'm not moving back into the bunkhouse."

"Very well. I believe that's something I can handle."

"When do I start?"

"Tonight would be nice," Helga said.